Photographic Memories

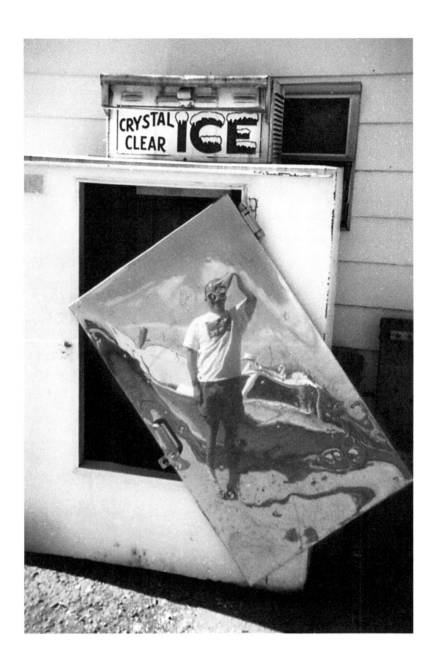

Photographic Memories

Selected Essays, Playlets, and Stories

Willy Conley

Gallaudet University Press

Washington, DC

Gallaudet University Press
gupress.gallaudet.edu

Gallaudet University Press is located on the
traditional territories of Nacotchtank and Piscataway.

ISBN 978-1-954622-13-5 (paperback)
ISBN 978-1-954622-14-2 (ebook)

Library of Congress Cataloging-in-Publication Data
Names: Conley, Willy, author.
Title: Photographic memories: selected essays, playlets, and stories /
    Willy Conley.
Description: Washington, DC: Gallaudet University Press, 2023. | Summary:
    "An anthology of essays, playlets, and short fiction"-- Provided by publisher.
Identifiers: LCCN 2022047947 (print) | LCCN 2022047948 (ebook) |
    ISBN 9781954622135 (paperback) | ISBN 9781954622142 (ebook)
Subjects: LCGFT: Essays. | Plays. | Short stories.
Classification: LCC PS3603.O536 P46 2023 (print) | LCC PS3603.O536
    (ebook) | DDC 811/.6--dc23/eng/20230124
LC record available at https://lccn.loc.gov/2022047947
LC ebook record available at https://lccn.loc.gov/2022047948

∞ This paper meets the requirements of ANSI/NISO Z39.48–1992
(Permanence of Paper).

Cover description: A photograph of a house's distorted reflection in a lake
with a partial grayscale filter. Overlaid are yellow and white text reading,
Photographic Memories Selected Essays Playlets and Stories. Below in
blue text reading, Willy Conley. Cover photo is titled "Little House on the
Suburban Prairie" and is credited, as all the other photos appearing in this
book, to Willy Conley. Used by permission.

For my father, Perry Lee, a.k.a. "Little Perry"

—you were always BIG Perry to me

What the Photograph reproduces to infinity has occurred only once: the Photograph mechanically repeats what could never be repeated existentially.

—Roland Barthes, *Camera Lucida*

Contents

Contents

Photographs

Preface

It seems that the number one hobby around the world these days is photography. Billions of photos are shot every day. Every year, 1.72 trillion photos are taken worldwide—that equals 54,400 snapshots per second (or 4.7 billion per day). By 2030, around 2.3 trillion photos will be taken every year; 92.5 percent of these photos will be shot by smartphones.[1] People are creating a tremendous number of photographic memories.

It all began in 1826 with the first known photograph, "View from the Window in Le Gras," taken by French inventor Joseph Nicéphore Niépce. In 1988, Fujifilm introduced the world to the first digital camera. Even though imaging technology developed rapidly at that point, photographs were not plentiful until digital cameras were installed in smartphones.[2] My first camera was a Ricoh 35 mm single lens reflex (SLR) that my parents bought for me when I was fourteen. An SLR is a what-you-see-is-what-you-get type of analog camera.

My father and I built a small darkroom near the basement steps of our house, and it was there that I spent many hours processing my first black-and-white images. From framing a scene in the camera's viewfinder, reading the light meter, setting the shutter speed, determining the f-stop, and pressing the shutter release, to winding the exposed film back into the canister, opening it in the dark, threading it onto a developing tank reel, mixing photo chemicals, processing the film, hanging the negative images up to dry, and then inserting them into the enlarger to create positive images onto photo paper, was a magical process to me. Watching an image slowly appear on paper under the amber illumination of a safelight was like the unwrapping of a Christmas gift; what gets revealed was always a surprise. The surprise came from remembering what was shot through the viewfinder and how the expectation of that mental image almost always turned

---

1. Matic Broz, "Number of Photos Statistics (2022)," *Photutorial* (March 10, 2022), https://photutorial.com/photos-statistics/.
2. Broz, "Number."

out different on film/paper. There is something about the latent image in the mind versus the one that ended up on film that created a sense of awe. Preeminent writer and philosopher Susan Sontag once said: "[Photographs are] not so much an instrument of memory as an invention of it or a replacement of it."[3]

I abhorred writing when I was a kid. Being the only deaf student in all-hearing public school classes, I barely got by stringing words together intelligibly enough to pass to the next grade. Instead, I learned to take good photographs before I could create good phrases. Basic Photography and Nature Photography were two of my favorite courses in high school. Besides physical education, they were the only courses that I earned an A in. This led to being selected to participate in a prestigious career development program during my senior year in high school. My career counselor found me a part-time job working for the pathology photography department at The Johns Hopkins Hospital in Baltimore. This valuable experience helped get me accepted into the undergraduate biomedical photography program at the Rochester Institute of Technology (RIT). It wasn't until I was enrolled there with other deaf students, along with teachers who used sign language, that my writing improved. I believe that as my access to ASL, my self-identity as a Deaf person, and my education grew, my ability to write strengthened.

During my junior year, I took a course from a deaf professor named Dr. Robert Panara. Back in the 1970s, he was the first deaf professor at RIT. He taught an intriguing class called Deaf Characters in Literature and Film. (If you ever want to know more about this magnificent human being and teacher, check out *Teaching from the Heart and Soul*.[4])

We studied different novels and films that had deaf characters in them, such as *Johnny Belinda*, *The Heart Is a Lonely Hunter*, and *In This Sign*. All were fascinating, well-written stories, but the one thing that stood out about them was that they were written by hearing writers whose observations of the Deaf experience were inauthentic or inaccurate.

---

3. Barbara F. Lefcowitz, "Memory and Photography," *Southwest Review* 96, no. 2 (2011): 231, http://www.jstor.org/stable/43473144.

4. Harry G. Lang, *Teaching from the Heart and Soul: The Robert F. Panara Story* (Washington, DC: Gallaudet University Press, 2007).

One of our assignments was to write a personal essay about a deaf experience we had. All of us in class looked at each other—"Deaf experience? What was that?" Dr. Panara taught us that it was whatever unique, odd, thought-provoking experience that impacted a deaf person in the hearing world. A brief example would be a deaf person going into a fast-food restaurant to order a burger, fries, and a soda. The deaf person gestures not being able to hear and that they would like a pen and paper to write down the order. The clerk would then hand over a braille menu. Everything that the deaf person had tried to gesture went completely out the window.

For the assignment, I started thinking about my own Deaf experiences. One that immediately stuck out in my head happened during a medical photography internship at Yale School of Medicine. One day I was called to the operating room to photograph open heart surgery— STAT! None of the other photographers were available. Usually, I knew in advance when I was scheduled to photograph surgery. I would meet surgeons ahead of time to let them know I was deaf and to come up with some simple hand signals for what type of photographs they wanted.

I wrote about this experience, which became my first essay involving creative writing. Dr. Panara gave me an A on the paper and encouraged me to submit it to *Symposium*, RIT's literary magazine at the time. *Symposium* decided to publish my story. Years later, I revised the story and had it published, along with a photograph of the human heart, in a national literary magazine. Seeing my own writing creations in black-and-white on the page enthralled me and spurred me on to write more. The very same feeling happened when I saw my first published photograph.

Sometimes a photo will trigger a memory that gives me a spark to ignite a story or a play. In my book *Vignettes of the Deaf Character and Other Plays*, there is a play (*The water falls.*) in the collection where the leitmotif is the reverberation of a grandfather's suicide among his family members.[5] I had a photograph of a rock impacting a still pond with ripples expanding outward. This image was the inspiration for my leitmotif.

---

5. Willy Conley, *Vignettes of the Deaf Character and Other Plays* (Washington, DC: Gallaudet University Press, 2009), 246–80.

Two plays in this collection had their beginnings created by photographs. Remains of Bosnians originated from my being greatly disturbed by images of genocide from the Bosnian War of 1992–1995. And in The Practice of Medicine, I used medical photographs to subtly protest how even in modern times doctors were still "practicing" their craft on live patients. This was my dramatic reaction to a personal experience of enduring the excruciating pain of retinal reattachment surgery.

One of the fascinating mysteries of writing for me is how I take small incidents from my life and expand upon them. I find it amazing how my mind takes me on a wild ride with where a character went or with what a character did. When I look back on a story I wrote, sometimes I am not sure how much of it was actually borrowed from my life. For instance, in "Every Man Must Fall," a story in this collection about how a fellow high school student/coworker's drowning deeply affected the main character, I based it on a real-life remembrance of the news about a high school classmate's drowning. Throughout my mid-teen years, I worked as a dishwasher at a local restaurant. What I could not remember was whether or not my classmate really worked with me. I thought to myself, "Wow—I made that up?" When rereading the story, the fiction I created felt so real to me.

Our memories may fade with time until we go back and review a photo of an event, after which the memory becomes refreshed. The incidents leading up to the event and of what happened after would come flooding back in the mind. But it is the exact moment recorded in the photograph that brings back a total recall with precision. (For an articulate, philosophical, and scholarly probe into the interrelation of memory and photography, the reader should explore Sontag's book On Photography.[6])

Sometimes we alter this memory with retouching to make it more romantic, aesthetic, cleaner, rosier, starker, more focused, better composed, less distracted, less traumatic, and so on. A photo accompanying a news article may be cropped for clarity, to allow for more writing space, or to channel the reader's gaze to a specific individual or object. Years ago, it was only the professionals who did the retouching of

---

6. Susan Sontag, On Photography (New York: Penguin, 2019).

photos. With the advent of Photoshop, Instagram, and other photo apps, anyone with a smartphone can manipulate their photographs and, hence, their memories.

During the summer of 1987 while on vacation at Deal Island, Maryland, I took a camera with me to do what we called in photo school "street shooting." It doesn't mean to go shooting with a gun in the streets but with a camera armed with film. The idea is to be ready to snap whatever catches one's eye. I found many subjects that were intriguing to shoot: dilapidated bait shacks, abandoned houses, cars rusting in a field, weathered boats, family graveyard plots, old churches. One day outside of a general store, I saw a run-down ice machine with its shiny door hanging askew. Seeing a reflection of myself on the door, I decided to take a self-portrait. A week later after the color slides were processed in a lab and sent to me, I discovered an image that captivated me. It was not a perfect mirror image of myself, but more reflective of the imperfect qualities of me: some rust on the machine, lettering with a retro style, and small dents in the metal door that gave it a warped look. I grew to like this self-portrait—not only for its representation of certain aspects of my personality, but also for its invocation of specific memories of that day when I went street shooting.

There is a so-called psychological or scientific phenomenon called "photographic memory," or "eidetic memory" as it is sometimes called. According to *New Scientist* magazine, people who have photographic memory indicate that they have the ability to recollect a past setting or situation in detail with precision. Even though a lot of people proclaim to have photographic memory, there is no scientific evidence of it. On the other hand, there is an ability called "highly superior autobiographical memory" (HSAM), where people can recall a past event in detail with a precise date of the occurrence. However, fewer than 100 people in the world have been recognized as having HSAM, and although their memories were outstanding, they were not as dependable as a photographic documentation.[7]

7. Alexandra McNamara and Matt Hambly, "Photographic Memory," *New Scientist* (May 25, 2021), https://www.newscientist.com/definition/photographic-memory/.

When an individual can clearly remember an image that they were briefly shown, it is called eidetic memory. For example, if a photo was revealed to someone, that person will continue to see the image for thirty seconds, sometimes even a few minutes after the photo was taken away.[8]

"A Photographic Memory," my autobiographical account of the open-heart surgery, was such a profound experience that it was burned into my memory. When I completed the operating room shoot, the image of the exposed, momentarily arrested heart flashed itself repeatedly in my head. At the time, I thought my precise reminiscence of it meant I had a photographic memory. And, when I wrote about this recollection a year later, it became a memory that I looked back on from time to time. Of course, over time, the memory was not quite exactly like the photo of the open heart I had taken on that extraordinary day.

The act of writing allows me to recall memories and shape them the way I like—much like a person taking a snapshot with their phone and retouching it to their personal tastes. The pieces in this volume are divided into three sections: essays, playlets, and stories. The essays involve a collection of published magazine articles, sidebars, dramaturgical pieces for stage production programs, and photo essays. The playlets—short, simple comedies and dramas—are grouped under *nonverbals*, meaning without spoken or signed language, and under *verbals*, referring to pieces involving spoken and signed language. Some of the stories are pieces that formed parts of my novel *The Deaf Heart*,[9] while others are stand-alone short fictions that were published in literary magazines and anthologies.

These selected, shaped works in written and visual form are my photographic memories.

Willy Conley
March 24, 2022

---

8. McNamara and Hambly, "Photographic Memory."
9. Willy Conley, *The Deaf Heart: A Novel* (Washington, DC: Gallaudet University Press, 2015).

Content Warning

References to audism, ableism, death, and animal abuse are present in the collection, as well as strong language. Readers who may be sensitive to these elements, please take note.

ESSAYS

The Honeybee Epiphany

People sometimes ask, "When did you first realize you were deaf?" It was an autumn afternoon in first grade. I felt a tickle behind my ear and brushed it away. I must have yelped because my teacher rushed over and pointed to a honeybee on the floor. I didn't understand. She gestured to take out my "things." I pulled out my hearing aids, which emitted high-pitched feedback. Everyone stared while she coated my whole ear with a paste of baking soda and water. I looked at the dying bee, not realizing that moment would be the beginning of many public school years of jeers about my deafness.

October 2008

Kindergarten to College

Make the most of every sense; glory in all facets of pleasure and beauty that the world reveals to you.

—Helen Keller, "The Seeing See Little"

I have been profoundly deaf since birth and, for seventeen years, grew up in an environment where everyone was hearing and where English was my first language. Consequently, my way of communicating with people developed by speaking and lipreading. As a junior in high school, I began looking into programs at nearby colleges (I had never heard of colleges for deaf students). Here I was, planning my future— a latent, culturally developed deaf person—bound to go through life with a strained smile, pretending to understand everything.

One day my parents and I went to The Johns Hopkins Hospital in Baltimore for my annual hearing test. After my audiologist heard that I was interested in further schooling, she advised me to look into the National Technical Institute for the Deaf at the Rochester Institute of Technology (NTID/RIT). A look through the institute's impressive catalog convinced my parents and me to drive to upstate New York to visit the campus. Our guide was deaf, and throughout the tour he signed, gestured, and used his voice and facial expressions, making explanations surprisingly easy for me to understand. Later, I learned that he used Total Communication, a language approach employed by the faculty and staff. I was amazed to find that NTID had an enrollment of more than 1,000 students, all of whom were deaf or hard of hearing. The support services offered—tutors, notetakers, and interpreters— were so luxurious compared to what I was getting in public schools, which was nothing. And to discover that I would be taught by professors who understood deafness—hallelujah! For the first time in my life— with the exception of kindergarten—I actually became excited about going to school.

Back home, I applied for the photography program at NTID/RIT, got accepted, and in the spring of 1976, finished high school being the only deaf graduate.

I never knew there were so many deaf people in America until I stood in the registration line for the Summer Vestibule Program, a four-week orientation for incoming deaf freshmen. All around me was a representative sampling of 250 deaf students from the four corners of the country. It was such a high that deep inside—corny as it may seem—I wanted to go up and hug each one and say, "Hi—I'm deaf too and have been waiting all my life to meet you."

During those five rich years that I lived on campus, my identity as a deaf individual began to surface. I discovered a part of myself that was missing for seventeen years: my roots in Deaf culture. The natural outcome was that sign language became my second language out of the need to fully understand my professors, classmates, and peers, both hearing and deaf.

Never again did I have to spend long hours straining my eyes to try and capture bits of information like I did in front rows of my early school years. Public school teachers often had their backs turned to the class while writing on the blackboard and lecturing—never mind how many times they were politely asked to face the front while talking. If I was lucky, I could read a word or two off their lips as they occasionally turned their heads sideways. When it came to class dis-cussions I was lost, stuck with a couple of words, trying to put together a fifty-piece puzzle that was missing forty-eight pieces.

But at NTID/RIT I was able to relax and enjoy my education. Either my instructors used sign language or I had an interpreter in front of me, allowing me to comprehend everything. A trained notetaker was nearby so I could fully concentrate on lectures and participate, una-bashedly, in discussions. A tutor who knew sign language was available if information in class became too complicated. In high school it was hard to find someone in class to volunteer to take notes for me. When that rare person was found, usually I couldn't read or understand their notes. Unlike my primary and secondary school years, I finally experi-enced the personal reward of high marks from postsecondary studies.

Soon I became friends with many people, people who signed and people who didn't—their preferences made no difference to me. It was such a novelty to make so many friends because up until the summer of 1976 I had very few, and never so many who were understand-ing and unbiased about deafness. It was so overwhelming that when my second year came around, I had to slap myself to remember the primary reason for being in college. A year of study had been completed at NTID's Applied Photography program, and I cross-registered to the School of Photographic Arts and Sciences to begin four years of study in biomedical photography. I did something that was painful—I cut back on a lot of friendships and socializing due to mounting academic pressures.

My academic routine was more manageable after two years at the school of photography. I was offered a position as a resident advisor for a special interest floor with all photography majors called Photo House, located in a predominantly deaf residence hall. I was very interested in being a part of a small floor community where the residents were deaf and hearing, and used photography as the basis to develop communication and relationships.

After a year with Photo House, I accepted a new challenge: to be an area administrative assistant for a predominantly hearing residence hall and resident adviser staff. My job was to assist the area director of the hall in the supervision of nineteen resident advisers as well as carry out the administrative duties for the housing office. Again, the interest was in encouraging deaf–hearing interaction using a higher, more visible position.

NTID has an incredible theatre program for not having theatre as a major. In their spare time, students along with faculty, staff, and members of the Rochester community presented well-crafted plays in sign language and voice. As my ability to understand the nuances of sign language became better, my appreciation for the theatre grew. I was finally being entertained by something other than a baseball game. Another form of entertainment that cropped up that I had been deprived of was captioned films. I was in heaven. I began to feel a fullness in my life—a balance where the weight of my social life equaled the weight of academia.

I developed an urge to be a part of the theatre and joined a resident troupe called Sunshine and Company. Part of the reason for joining was the desire to be a communicator; to convey artistic images and ideas to people just like I had seen the actors do on stage. Another part was to instill confidence in myself with my new language and newfound identity.

My entire college education was served to me like a sumptuous feast. It was all there in clear view and within reach, and I consumed it. On graduation day, I was literally twenty pounds overweight and satisfied.

In different cities around the country where I worked, I ran into deaf people, young and old, who seemed to try awfully hard to be like "normal hearing people." They had darting eyes and nervous smiles. When I said something, often they nodded their heads but said, "Huh? What?" It pained me to see this because I sensed something they were not aware was missing from their lives; a void that I used to have. I wanted to blurt out the news about Deaf culture, the many clubs and organizations of the deaf, the theatres of the deaf, and the deaf sports teams and competitions. I wanted to tell them about literature and films with deaf characters and writers, show them art by deaf artists and, ultimately, introduce them to another language, rich and . . . at last, attainable.

But sometimes I held back because of overprotective parents who hovered close by—parents who were adamant about their child not coming in contact with sign language or Deaf culture for fear that their child will lose—of all things—their speech.

Or, sometimes I hesitated because some deaf people were so proud of their speech and success in the hearing world that they didn't need to be involved with Deaf culture and sign language.

It horrifies me to think where I would be today if I had not gone to a college for the deaf.

Years later, some people can't understand my drastic career change from biomedical photography to professional acting. I think there's a parallel between photographers and actors in that both are communicators of ideas and images. The biomedical photographer's job is to record medical facts on film and communicate them in a factual, visual way for doctors who need to present these facts in journals, conventions, lectures, and grand rounds. The actor's job is to absorb a playwright's text and communicate it in an accurate, artistic way to an audience. But "Why the career jump?" my friends ask. Why not? I had passed rigorous requirements to be certified as a Registered Biological Photographer and, during a span of seven years, I worked diligently for some of the top hospitals in the world—Hopkins, Yale,

University of Texas Medical Branch, and Cedars-Sinai. It was time for a change—to delve into the unknown and further explore my potential in life.

If it wasn't for my parents' unselfish support and sacrifice to get me through college, I never would have been able to do the things I have done. I am at the five-year mark working as a full-time actor, and today I am learning to write.

1991

The Face of Grace

In 1984 I served a two-week rotation in clinical photography as part of my internship at the University of Texas Medical Branch in Galveston. I needed the experience of photographing live human subjects as opposed to dead cells under a microscope or body parts in the morgue. The biomedical photo department arranged one day each semester to shoot yearbook photographs of students in the medical field. Hundreds of faces paraded through the studio. "Sit here. Straighten your back. Tilt your head. Smile!"

Then, this nursing student walked in with a real smile. "Hi, I'm Grace." I found her easy to lipread and hear with my hearing aids on. Her lips, tongue, and teeth wrapped themselves perfectly around words. Grace sat on the stool and instinctively knew how to pose.

I snapped a few frames, and mustered the nerve to say, "Stop by the studio and visit us again." A week later she came by and asked if I'd like to get together for a barbecue on the beach. Her lips puckered at the end of "barbecue." After work, I rushed over to Grace's house on my bike only to find that it was her father's house and that he and her brother were coming along.

"Oh, great . . . swell, bring them along," I said. I had such good social graces. We rode in her Mercedes convertible over the hard-packed sand and parked a few feet away from the Gulf. It was a beautiful November evening with the temperatures still in the upper seventies. Grace's father and brother lit up the hibachi while she and I threw a Frisbee around. Grace told me that her father was an orthopedic surgeon. Her brother worked for the Coast Guard.

By the time the hot dogs and baked beans were cooked, it was past dusk. I sat on a rock munching on my hot dog. I looked over at Grace sitting across from me. Her face was just a dark silhouette. I couldn't see her lips or her smile. I couldn't talk.

Back at her father's house, we sipped coffee in awkward silence. Her father asked me, "Do you go to church?"

"Uh, no. Not really."

"I see. Well, Grace, time for me to go to bed. Goodnight y'all."

I said goodnight to them all, riding away on my bike with the framed image of Grace's blue eyes and smile forever etched in my mind.

December 2006

Human Sign Language

Being profoundly deaf, I need to use American Sign Language (ASL) to communicate in my daily life. ASL is a three-dimensional, mobile, visual language, which is not written or spoken. During my travels in America, it is seldom that I meet other people who know ASL, so communication with people who can hear is often inaccessible or difficult, unless I write back and forth with them in English on paper. What I have come to appreciate are symbols or written English language on signs in the American landscape. Handwritten, manufactured, or printed text are little windows of access where I understand the language of a particular environment, no matter how coherent, incoherent, congruous, or incongruous it may be.

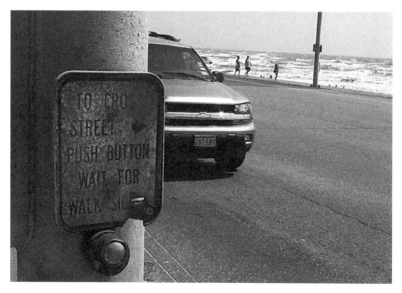

The Power of Salt Air

Old Hearing Privilege

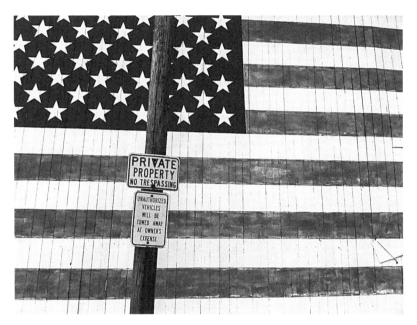

Small Town Territorialism

Dashed Field of Dreams

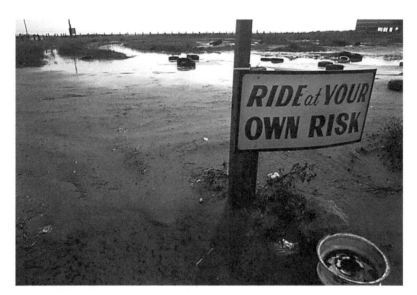

Old Go-Kart Track

Fall 2012

Day 57
—on the road with the National Theatre of the Deaf

Nat Wilson, Sandi Inches, Andy Vasnick, and Adrian Blue chat during a rest stop.

Production stage manager, Fred Noel, on the mobile phone with the home office.

Destination: Memphis, Tennessee—480 miles

Three men hold machine guns and pistols point-blank at the bus driver's head. Bandannas pulled up to their eyes, arms outstretched, and fingers on the triggers, the hijackers stare down at the uniformed man. They wait for a response. The driver casually shifts gears and then adjusts his side view mirror.

Adjacent to the holdup is a man with an open briefcase on his lap; schedules are scattered on the seat next to him. He doodles on a legal pad and talks business through a mobile phone, gripping the receiver with his head and shoulder. When he looks up, the receiver drops on the floor. His eyes and mouth widen.

One of the armed men gestures toward the speedometer.

"Is this as fast as you can go?"

"Yeah, step on it, man!"

The driver's frame is like an anchor, heavy and resistant to onrushing currents. Once on Main Street in a small mining town in the Blue Ridge mountains, he pulls the bus over for a rest stop. When he gets out to stretch, people slow down and stare at his size. Unfazed, he says to them, "Whatsa matter—ain't you ever seen a bus before?"

The driver chuckles. He maintains his speed and steers the bus with one hand comfortably on the wheel.

"C'mon, you want your brains splattered all over the windshield?" said a hijacker.

Silence.

In a burst of firepower, the guns squirt jets of water on the windshield, the driver's arms, and his bus-blue tie. He lets out a great laugh, not even swerving the bus out of its lane. The three men take their bandannas off. They laugh and pat the driver on the back.

"You're cool, Al. You stay awake now."

On Interstate 45 the bus carries a cargo of twelve actors and two stage technicians (the other two technicians are hours ahead of us, heading for the next theatre, in a rental truck with the play's set). An actor presses his face against the cool window and watches the yellow dashes chase each other down the center of the highway. Out of the corner of his eye, he notices a piece of tape flapping in the wind. One of the actors had cut professional-looking letters, "NATIONAL THEATRE OF THE DEAF" along the side of the bus using a razor knife and black gaffer's tape. The bus is chartered by the National Theatre of the Deaf for the entire season and he felt our company deserved a little recognition on the road. The actor staring out the window sees that the peeling tape is the letter "F" from the word DEAF. He grins at the thought of people driving by thinking they're some morbid theatre of the dead.

The barren east Texas landscape floats by like driftwood even though the bus is going sixty-five. I stand to stretch a crick in my neck and my head bumps on the luggage shelf. I turn and look down the aisle at the people I work with. Across from me is an actor who takes advantage of every free moment to sleep. Most mornings she sleepwalks to the bus from her hotel room. Her gray backpack, stuffed to the seams, looms over behind her, its weight guiding her toward the waiting bus. She has worked out a deal with her roommate. On days that she sleepwalks, he takes care of her half of the hotel bill with the understanding that she'll pay him back when she wakes up. Often, she wakes up just when we arrive at the next hotel. Now she is bundled in a ball like a cat, eyes closed, probably practicing her favorite pastime: an out-of-body experience.

Every other pair of reclining seats on the bus has been taken out to provide more leg room and storage for the actors. The married couples have their seats set up to face each other; they decorate the space between them as if it were home. A husband-and-wife team of ten years sits opposite each other. The decor of their space has a set of curtains with frills, shelving with books, motor mugs and thermos, an ice chest that serves as a coffee-lunch-card table and cold storage, flowers in a vase, photographs taped to the window, fruits and vegetables in a basket, and pillows and blankets. The husband casually studies configurations in a Japanese dictionary. His wife bites her fingernails while engrossed in a Danielle Steel novel.

Next to them is another couple asleep with a teddy bear embraced between them. Behind these two is an actor engaged in the daily routine of developing his biceps with a twenty-five-pound dumbbell. He lifts the weight with one hand while reading *Lonesome Dove* from the other; he's quite good at turning pages with one hand.

A tall actor with a scraggly beard and long stringy hair leans against the door of the occupied bathroom; an unlit cigarette dangles from his mouth. Our contracts have a clause that says we absolutely cannot change our appearance until the show ends for the season. The day after a show closes, everyone dashes off to a hair salon to shed their old appearance.

The scruffy actor's feet cross and uncross, and his hands scramble for something loose in his pockets. Suddenly he bangs on the door with his boot heel to get the bathroom occupant to hurry up. Smoking in the open is forbidden. Smokers must resort to puffing through a small window in the bathroom next to the toilet. He complains that the bus smells like a roadside portable toilet.

A burly, gray-bearded actor is in such deep concentration that his tongue has worked its way out of his mouth trying to escape the intense focus. He glues together the parts of a biplane model. Diagrams, balsa wood chips, straight pins, and dried strands of toxic-smelling glue are all over his living area.

In the front just behind the driver, an actor dressed in running gear balances a bowl of Grape Nuts on his lap. He reaches into his cooler—which doubles as a footrest—for a pint of milk. To save our health, and a little per diem, some of us avoid fast food restaurants by purchasing fresh groceries.

When I joined the National Theatre of the Deaf three years ago as an actor, I soon discovered why we're still around after twenty-two years, which is more than most American touring theatre companies. We practice the oldest theatrical tradition: traveling. The more we travel and perform, the more people we reach; the more money we earn to sustain another year, the more places we can return to perform again. We do not perform solely for deaf audiences but for all audiences. A controversial fact is that our theatregoers are predominantly hearing. Our detractors claim it's because our brand of theatre is too highbrow to draw a large deaf turnout. Therefore, our work is most appealing to hearing people. Our proponents dispute that there are lots of theatres that produce plays too intellectual for hearing people and say that roughly 10 percent of the US population attend plays. So, take 10 percent of the US deaf population and you'll understand why theatre houses aren't always filled with deaf people.

But someone will counter, "What's with all that flowery sign language and exaggerated movement? Deaf people don't do that. And who's gonna pay ten to fifteen bucks to see that when we can use the money to get in a bowling tournament, drink all the beer we want, and after the games, watch a stripper in the bowling lanes?"

There must be something wrong with people who pay $50.00 to see Hamlet utter eloquent, complicated phrases not used today. Isn't that what art is all about—something a person over time acquires a taste for, like a Picasso painting or a sixteen-year-old bottle of imported Lagavulin Scotch whisky?

A petition slowly zigzags down the aisle pausing for people to read and sign. It's a letter of protest to a major network berating them for hiring a hearing actress in a deaf role on prime time TV. I sign it, concluding a full list of signatures, and slip it back into the envelope addressed to CBS Television. The bus is now awake with actors hotly discussing the new topic of the day. Here were twelve strongly emotional people—paid to project emotions—all with excellent arguments against CBS, demonstrating up and down the aisle of a bus with dark-tinted windows. We had to be content with the knowledge that we were increasing deaf awareness and promoting deaf rights in our own discreet, indirect way of theatre.

The National Theatre of the Deaf produces one two-hour main-stage production per year. The biggest challenge of a long tour is to keep the show alive, night after night, as if we were performing for the first time. Every night when the lights hit us, each actor had better be out on stage giving 100 percent; that includes performing with a broken nose, during birthdays and holidays, or with a 102-degree fever from an exotic insect bite. There are no understudies, and the only thing that stops us is deathly illness, or a cancelation by the people sponsoring the show. Recently, for the first time in our twenty-two-year history, our play was aborted midway through the first act by an ultraconservative religious college. The play had some so-called obscenities (*damn, hell, screw, manhood,* possibly *pimple*) and sexual undertones. We're not deaf and angelic; we're deaf and human.

Someone has just taped a drawing of the Trojan horse to the bus ceiling. An actor stands blindfolded underneath the horse with a cut-out photograph in his hand of another actor's head—the actor who played Odysseus, the lead role. The photograph is small, round, and replaces the proverbial donkey's tail. It really is an a— ... it's an obscure body part that my father calls an "a. h." The actor is spun around in the aisle several times before she "pins" the horse. Everyone howls when she sticks the little photograph on the emergency exit hatch.

On an eight-week tour we sometimes work continuously for fourteen days, taking breaks only to travel, eat, and sleep. Occasionally, when the stars aren't right, we find ourselves in a poorly managed budget motel with a picturesque name like Quail Lakes Lodge. It's a visual oxymoron. We're stuck at an interstate junction with nothing around but farmland and a truck stop. The beds are rickety, the water is as brown as the plowed fields, and phone numbers for a good time are scrawled on the back of Gideon bibles.

When the stars are aligned, we get the red-carpet treatment. Don't laugh. One day we rolled up the driveway of a hotel somewhere in the Midwest, and on the lawn nearby sat a welcoming committee of four women. As soon as the bus opened its door, two women came up to the bus steps and unrolled a red carpet all the way to the hotel's entrance. A woman stood to the side of the carpet with a basket of polished red apples. The other woman stayed behind at the table with our room keys all laid out in neat, numerical order. As each one of us stepped off the bus, we were greeted with a warm hug, an apple, and a key.

Sometimes we'll arrive at a theatre where the stage is extremely small, forcing the technical crew to leave out parts of the set. As a result, a dance number may have to be rechoreographed, or some scenes may need to be reblocked. Some of us may have to figure out new visual cues for stage entrances and exits. The list of last-minute problems can go on, but the name of the game is flexibility—a quality that literally builds character in all of us.

Occasionally, people at receptions or at question-and-answer sessions ask if we're paid Broadway scale for all the work and travel we do. No, we live comfortably on our pay; however, being stage actors, we learn to scrape pennies.

When friends come backstage, they envision sparkling clean, well-lit dressing rooms with our names under a gold star on the door. Usually, they'll find three or four actors hopping around trying to slip into their costumes in a tiny, dust-laden room with a few burned-out light bulbs. The modest lose their modesty quickly; there's not much say about where, and in front of whom, we change our clothes. What about fans pouring in backstage demanding autographs? Not really the case, though we get the occasional brave soul who doesn't think deaf people will bite.

Why bother with this grueling career? Some actors have chosen it because they say the theatre is the best teacher of life. I remember an actor telling me once that he loves being the communicator. He sculpts the playwright's text with his hands, gives it to the audience, and sees them take it into their hands in the form of applause. Another actor remarked that she craves the theatre because it offers a juncture where the mind, body, and spirit intersect and work.

The bus swerves hard onto the right shoulder, kicking up a dust storm. Al, the driver, leans over and scrutinizes the side-view mirror. He swears he heard a police siren, but a patrol car is nowhere to be seen. Cruising up the aisle is a shiny, diminutive black-and-white car with a revolving red dome light. A small crowd at the back of the bus has gathered around the company wiseacre. He guides his toy car by remote control up to Al's feet. A note is taped to the hood: "You awake, Al?"

After the laughter and backslapping subsides, the bus rolling once again, I sit down to work on a crossword puzzle. My neck feels a little better now and I'm more aware of the luggage shelf above me. Before I begin on the first clue, I think a moment about why I love this company . . . . I think it's because when we travel far from our own families, we become a surrogate family; a family that laughs, fights, cries, and loves one another like brothers and sisters. After all, we're in the same bus.

Fall 1990

From Lipreading Ants to Flying over Cuckoo Nests

I hated theatre when I was growing up. One of my earliest memories is seeing an outdoor production of *The Lost Colony* in North Carolina. I was deaf (still am) and couldn't hear the dialogue. To make matters worse, my parents and I were seated so many rows back in the amphitheater that the actors were practically the size of ants on stage. Try lipreading an ant. I vaguely recall a lot of little figures in colorful historical costumes standing around in front of a stockaded background with some cannons going off. The booming cannons and smoke held my attention. We left in the middle of the show, not because I couldn't understand a damn thing on stage but because some lady sitting behind us threw up on my mother's back. Years later in college at the National Technical Institute for the Deaf (NTID) in Rochester, New York, I finally understood my first play—a sign language production of *One Flew over the Cuckoo's Nest* with all deaf actors. I was struck by the poignancy of life in an insane asylum, with the subtext of how deaf people were once thought of as being dumb or crazy. The passionate expressions of deaf actors using American Sign Language (ASL) moved me. As I attended more and more sign language plays, my appreciation grew for my Deaf culture and the theatre. I fell in love with the theatre and have been in love ever since.

Upon graduation, I worked in various places around the country during the 1980s and '90s, hardly finding any sign language plays or deaf actors wherever I went. If I was lucky, I could catch a deaf theatre company on tour or a community production in sign language once or twice a year. Usually, I would have to drive over a hundred miles or fly somewhere. If nothing was happening, I went to see hearing plays, which were everywhere. Very few were sign-interpreted; most turned out to be static, with talking heads against pretty backdrops. I kept thinking how theatrical deaf actors were, naturally filling the stage space with ASL along with their inherent physical and emotional qualities—and how invisible they were as a culture and as theatre artists. What would it take for them to be more visible and invincible in American theatre?

As a deaf theatre artist who now works in both professional and university theatre, I believe that the potential for growth, recognition, and employment is vast for deaf theatre and its artists. Watching African American, Hispanic American, and Asian American theatre artists come of age in the entertainment industry, I sense that our time will come, too. However, that will not happen unless deaf theatre artists regroup and make a concerted, driven effort to achieve a standard of excellence that equals or goes beyond the level of professional hearing theatre.

Considerable progress has been made toward that standard, beginning with the mother of all Deaf theatres, the Tony Award–winning National Theatre of the Deaf (NTD), a touring company established in Connecticut in 1967. There are other full-time professional and semiprofessional theatre companies: the Fairmount Theatre of the Deaf (now called Cleveland Signstage Theatre), the first resident deaf company in the country; Sunshine Too National Touring Company, an educational outreach troupe of NTID; and the award-winning Deaf West Theatre, a regional company in Los Angeles that is the youngest and fastest-growing sibling.

Before we look at what standard of excellence needs to be established or what efforts need to be made to create more visibility, we should examine our natural resources. One is deaf children, who express the experience of their world through gestures, mimicry, and movement based on innate rhythms, drawings, and paintings. In their text *International Visual Theatre Research Community*, Jean Grémion and Maurice McClelland noticed that "deaf children can do more precise imitations of people they meet briefly than most trained mimes. It is in fact through this kind of imitation that they 'describe' who a person is to each other."[1]

Grémion and McClelland also observed that deaf people's intense reliance on visual perception is a "moment-to-moment reality." Because subtle facial expressions and body movements are the foundations of sign language, deaf people often have a heightened ability

---

1. Jean Grémion and Maurice McClelland, *International Visual Theatre Research Community*, (Paris: International Theatre Institute, 1976), 33.

to "read" human relationships, particularly in watching what hearing people's faces and bodies reveal during social encounters.

Deaf people also have an increased sense of spatial awareness, the writers observed. Therefore, it almost goes without saying that a deaf actor naturally creates a visual theatre environment with the use of the entire body as means of communication, especially when communicating in ASL. Imagine the theatre space around a deaf actor being filled by arm, hand, body, and face movements. Imagine further exploring this space by exaggerating and heightening ASL the way hearing playwrights would do with the English language; then, add stage business or movement in conjunction with ASL. Already, a large amount of that empty stage space gets utilized or covered by movement.

I teach at Gallaudet University, the world's only four-year liberal arts college for deaf people. Large numbers of our students have good physical, gestural, and movement skills and the potential to capitalize on them. Many have a natural command of their facial expressions, their bodies, and their language—ASL. Most are quite creative in this respect. But when encouraged to consider a theatre career or take more theatre courses beyond the customary Introduction to Theatre, most will decline. They say that either vocational rehabilitation (VR) or their parents will not support such a decision. The parents or VR counselors must assume that there's no market for deaf theatre artists: If theatre is extremely competitive for hearing people, then the competition has to quadruple for deaf people. Some of our graduates will go on to find nine-to-five jobs, performing skits or one-person shows at Deaf community events during their spare time. Others will just let their natural theatre skills fall by the wayside.

As sad as it is to see all this wasted talent, it is even more discouraging in light of the amazing number of hearing actors who are weak in the use of their faces and bodies, but have nevertheless carved out a substantial career in the theatre. What they get by on is standing in costume looking interesting and having that almost holy ability to speak the English language to those who adore hearing it, never mind how limited or awkward the movements on stage.

David Hays, the hearing founder of the National Theatre of the Deaf, remarked, "To me, there is something inexpressive, stilted, and almost boring about the hearing actor opening and closing a little hole in the lower middle of his face. Wonderful, meaningful noise emerges, but if only he could do that with his arms, his knees, his shoulders, his fingers—and have his full face not just 'in support' but as something read. And with signing, every part of the body works to inflect color, to tilt the word toward full emotional meaning."[2]

It is strange that most professional theatres shy away from the visual potential of incorporating ASL and deaf actors on the stage. Is it because of the predominantly hearing audience? Fear of the unknown, of people who are different? In her book *Theatre Games for the Classroom*, Viola Spolin has an audience-involvement exercise called "Deaf Audience." Its focus is physically "communicating a scene to a deaf audience."[3] It might be good for the hearing audience as well. The idea is not to dumb down the material, of course, but to find creative ways to make it visually accessible to all audiences regardless of language backgrounds. And in the process, why not employ some deaf actors who can do this well? Spolin's "Deaf Audience" ought to be called "Playing to a Global Audience." There must be something inherently intriguing about watching a performance without spoken language.

In a *US News & World Report* article, the director Peter Sellars made an apt remark: "There is an extra dimension in the work of deaf actors, who are aware of the miracle of getting an idea across."[4] He would know. Sellars is one of those rare and daring directors who is not afraid to work with deaf theatre artists. Not only did he cast a deaf actor, Howie Seago, in *Ajax* and *The Persians* during the 1980s, he also collaborated with deaf playwright Shanny Mow in a 1981 NTD production of *The Ghost of Chastity Past, or The Incident at Sashimi Junction.*[5] Regarding this collaboration, Mow, who is of Chinese

---

2. Stephen C. Baldwin, *Pictures in the Air: The Story of the National Theatre of the Deaf* (Washington, DC: Gallaudet University Press, 1992).
3. Viola Spolin, *Theatre Games for the Classroom* (Evanston, IL: Northwestern University Press, 1986).
4. Alvin P. Sanoff, "The Power of Unspoken Words (Deaf Actors in Plays and Movies)," *US News & World Report*, 101 (1986): 83–84.
5. Willy Conley, "A Play of Our Own."

descent, commented that since Sellars grew up in Japan, he was the perfect collaborator for this play, with its Kabuki-Western motif.

Another bold director, Robert Wilson, has also worked with deaf actors. In 1988 at the Brooklyn Academy of Music, he cast Seago in *The Forest* (based on *The Epic of Gilgamesh*) in the role of Enkido, the story's hero. In one of Wilson's early theatre works, *The King of Spain*, he cast a young, deaf African American actor named Raymond Andrews, who later became the director's inspiration for the much-acclaimed *Deafman Glance*. About Andrews, Wilson remarked that people "thought the child was a freak or an idiot, [but] he's developed another sense of seeing-hearing that's very amazing."[6] Wilson is particularly interested in developing theatre pieces with individuals who have been restricted in their use of verbal language and have "compensated for this by developing awarenesses and sensitivities to non-verbal channels of communication that go unnoticed by people who use verbal language regularly."[7]

Mark Medoff is another venturesome hearing theatre artist who has collaborated with deaf actors. After he wrote the landmark play *Children of a Lesser God*, inspired by the life story of deaf actress Phyllis Frelich, Medoff created for her the substantial role of Marieta, a deaf playwright in *The Hands of Its Enemy*. Recently, Frelich and Medoff have collaborated on Medoff's new plays *Gila* and *A Christmas Carousel*, which include yet more characters for Frelich to perform.

Michael Kahn, artistic director of the Shakespeare Theatre in Washington, DC, has cast several deaf actors in his productions over the past decade, including Warren Snipe in the role of Puck in a Shakespeare-in-the-Park production of *A Midsummer Night's Dream*; Mary Vreeland as Katrin in *Mother Courage and Her Children* (for which she won a Helen Hayes Award in 1992); and, most recently, for his September 1999 production of *King Lear*, Monique Holt as

---

6. Stefan Brecht, *The Theatre of Visions: Robert Wilson* (Frankfurt: Suhrkamp, 1978), 429.

7. Jerrold A. Phillips, "Strategies of Communication in Recent Experimental Theatre," in *Proceedings of the Speech Communication Association Convention*, November 4, 1978, Minneapolis, MN, https://eric.ed.gov/?q=Jerrold+A.+Phillips&id=ED165212.

Cordelia, along with another deaf actor, Stella Antonio-Conley, as her understudy.

Nick Olcott, a freelance theatre artist mostly associated with Round House Theatre in Maryland, directed a daring and ground-breaking deaf/hearing production of *The Miracle Worker* at Arena Stage in Washington, DC, in early 2000. He dared to put signing deaf actors in a theatre in the round. (Imagine solving sight-line problems to ensure that an audience has an unobstructed view of actors using ASL!) Olcott broke ground, literally and figuratively, by digging out "foxholes" at the four corners of the stage and putting a signing actor in each one as a kind of witness to all that was spoken on stage. The most authentic aspect of the production was casting deaf actor Shira Grabelsky in the role of Helen Keller.

It is wonderful that these well-known artists, knowingly or not, con-tribute to upgrading the status of deaf theatre artists. It is, however, worth noting that not one deaf director or playwright has yet been allowed the opportunity to make such contributions in commercial theatre.

Certainly, a rich vein of deaf theatre and its artists is being qui-etly and hesitantly chipped into, but no one is rushing in to dig out the mother lode. It's disheartening to see deaf theatre artists some-times employed for one-time, pet projects of hearing theatre artists. A nagging thought persists regarding the use of deaf actors for one-shot deals: Are deaf actors being exploited for mere spectacle? Those mentioned above should be lauded for their ongoing commitment to employ deaf theatre artists.

For deaf theatre artists to take advantage of their potential, they must address these and other issues and explore possibilities for improvement. Critical and more appropriate standards of evaluation must be applied to their work, particularly when virtually no eval-uators or reviewers have any background in sign language or Deaf culture.

Sometimes, deaf playwrights wonder what hearing theatres and solicitors of play scripts think when they receive a script that calls for deaf characters. Are they thinking, "Well, not a bad script, but we have no deaf actors or directors in our theatre who can workshop this. None of the actors on file or in our company know signs." How many scripts by deaf playwrights have been turned down with this reasoning? Shouldn't these decision-makers be up on the Non-Traditional Casting Project in New York City, which has huge online files on artists of color and those who are differently abled? And what about Ken Elks's Deaf Entertainment Guild in Beverly Hills? He has a website listing deaf and hard of hearing theatre artists. Word needs to get out about these avenues of access and availability.

How can theatre critics in the media accurately review a sign language production if they don't know ASL? Many try to hide their ignorance with timeworn clichés like, "The sign language was absolutely beautiful—silent poetry in the air." For all they know, a deaf actor may have flubbed lines or could be merely moving his or her hands around in a manual gibberish to make it look like something significant was being signed. I know—as an actor I've done this, and have seen others do it, too.

While deaf theatre artists are thus denied access to knowledgeable and professional adjudication, they face a subtler barrier to evaluation when they become intoxicated by the applause of their peers. When a sign language show does come to town, deaf people drink it all in with little complaint about quality or flavor. But now seems to be the time for deaf theatre and its artists to rise above the level of mediocrity and stop being too pleased with what they've been doing.

First, we should look at where we've been. Deaf theatre artists seldom get the opportunity to be exposed to works outside their own small circle. This isn't entirely their fault, of course, because as an audience member it is difficult to watch hearing plays—most are completely inaccessible. Hearing theatre artists get to see lots of theatre anytime, anywhere. They don't even have to read a script before seeing a play!

Certainly, some hearing theatre performances are visually rich or nonverbal enough to be worth the time and ticket price for a deaf audience. In these cases, however, the problem lies with the Deaf community having no way of knowing when and where such shows exist. Many deaf people have been "burned" from attending highly verbal and visually static performances time and again, and have simply stopped following production notices. To address this problem,

I propose that theatre marketing departments latch onto a theatre-savvy Deaf community liaison and use this person to tap into the Deaf network. Theatres can give the liaison a complimentary ticket or entry to a rehearsal for upcoming shows, which that person can then review for the Deaf community.

Sign interpretation of spoken plays has been the most widely known technique for making performances accessible to deaf people in the United States—yet contrary to popular belief, simply providing sign language interpreting does not create equal access for deaf audiences. Interpreters are usually placed off to the side of the stage, where they sit or stand immobile in a small spotlight and translate the spoken text to the deaf audience during performances created chiefly for the hearing audience—that is to say, with a focus on speech rather than movement. For deaf audiences, watching a sign-interpreted show is much like reading a script—with their eyes darting back and forth between the interpreter and the actors. The rich language of the playwright gets watered down and the subtleties in acting, directing, and design become lost.

It must be said in favor of sign-interpreted theatre that it works very well when a play is light in verbosity, has strong visual elements, and the interpreters are in good position in correlation to the stage and the deaf audience—and when they are well-coached by a sign master, a deaf consultant knowledgeable in theatre and sign translation.

An important, positive side effect of sign-interpreted performances is that it gives the hearing audience exposure to ASL, which spills over to create some appreciation of deaf people and their culture. The downside is that the interpreters sometimes get all of the credit for creating this beautiful "language in the air" because they are the ones in that little spotlight off to the side of the stage.

Instead of expecting theatre to provide interpreted shows, it would be great to use this money instead for rehearsal interpreters in order to put deaf actors *on the stage*. This would guarantee a steady subscription from a deaf audience, rather than the sporadic attendance we have now. Oftentimes I've been begged to come to a performance because no deaf people were expected to show up for a scheduled interpreted show. It's humiliating, not to mention a sheer waste of time and money for interpreters and sign masters who've already translated and rehearsed the script. Shanny Mow told me once that the Americans with Disabilities Act should not be about trying to give deaf people access to hearing theatre—it should be the other way around: giving the hearing access to *us*. Change their attitude, not ours—we're fine.[8]

An obviously important aspect of a deaf theatre artist's growth is education and training. Theatre conservatories and university programs have to be more open to the idea of allowing enrollment of deaf theatre students. How else would these aspiring theatre artists improve their craft other than going out on their own and learning on the job?

An example of failure to level the playing field between deaf and hearing theatre artists happened in 1989 when I applied for the MFA playwriting program at the Yale School of Drama. David Hays, the former Broadway lighting and set designer, and Dennis Scott, the late chair of Yale's graduate directing program (who had traveled to New York City to see a play of mine off-off Broadway), wrote glowing letters of recommendation to go with my application. I was invited for an interview with Milan Stitt, the playwriting chair. For political reasons, I decided not to bring an interpreter along—it might make me look too dependent and needy. Despite some illegal, personal questions (such as "How did you become deaf?"), Stitt and I seemed to really hit it off. A few weeks later I received a personal letter from Stitt, the principal tenet of which was the unfortunate comment that "we do not feel you have quite found your 'voice.'"

Thanks to Hays's guidance, within a year I was accepted into Derek Walcott's graduate playwriting program at Boston University. Walcott shared his phenomenal sense of poetry, playwriting, and humor with me in class and over occasional dinners. Toward the completion of my degree, he produced a one-act play of mine at his Boston Playwrights Theatre. I left the program with a master of arts degree, feeling proud and respected.

It's easy to imagine the struggles that other aspiring deaf theatre artists face when they want to enroll in a theatre degree program. For those interested, the following universities have been known to

---

8. Shanny Mow, personal interview, April 21, 1998.

accept deaf students into their drama programs: American University, Arizona State University, Boston University, California State University at Northridge, Catholic University, Connecticut College, New York University, SUNY Purchase, Towson University, University of Maryland, University of Texas at Austin, and Wesleyan University (Connecticut), as well as, of course, Gallaudet University.

Maybe it's time to pull out the affirmative action card—if it's done in the regular workplace, it ought to be done in the arts place. *The Gallaudet Encyclopedia of Deaf People and Deafness* contains this unfortunate fact: "No play with a deaf theme written by a deaf playwright has been produced by commercial theatre."[9] That was published in 1987 and is still true today.

If there's a single area that needs a blow from the hammer of affirmative action to keep the competition fair and square, it is casting. For any deaf role that needs to be filled in theatre, film, or television, cast a deaf actor, not a hearing one. Hollywood has a horrendous reputation for casting hearing actors in deaf roles. The theatre is guilty of the same thing. David Hays put it succinctly: "Casting performers who can hear in deaf roles is like putting a white actor in black-face to play Othello."[10] Phyllis Frelich gave an impassioned presentation at the 1984 American Theatre Association convention about hearing actors still being cast to play deaf roles in various offshoot productions of *Children of a Lesser God*, despite the playwright's insistence that "in *any* professional production of this play, the roles of Sarah, Orin, and Lydia [all deaf] be performed by deaf or hearing-impaired actors."[11] So why do hearing directors still cast hearing actors for deaf roles?

Roles for deaf actors do not get publicized like those for the hearing in issues of *Daily Variety*, *Drama-logue*, or *Backstage*, so deaf actors are not likely to regularly read the trades. Besides, casting agents generally don't want to bother with deaf theatre artists—it's the old saw, "They're not marketable."

---

9. John Van Cleve, *Gallaudet Encyclopedia of Deaf People and Deafness* (New York: McGraw Hill, 1987), 291.

10. Alvin P. Sanoff, "The Power of Unspoken Words (Deaf Actors in Plays and Movies)," *US News & World Report* 101 (1986).

11. Mark Medoff, *Children of a Lesser God* (New York: Dramatist Play Service, 1980).

My own experience suggests that the only way to break into the mainstream of professional theatre, gain artistic and management experience, and raise standards for deaf theatre is through collaboration. There is a growing trend of deaf theatre artists being invited to become associate artists at regional theatres, but this comes after these artists were aggressive and aware enough to find ways to put their foot in the proverbial backstage door. My invitation to become an associate artist at Center Stage in Baltimore stemmed from a connection with Denise Gantt, a fellow MFA theatre student at Towson University. In a dramaturgy class Gantt and I were taking, she announced one day that Center Stage, where she worked as director of Theatre for a New Generation, was interested in reading new plays for a possible staged reading of graduate writings. I gave her my latest play, which ended up being selected. Irene Lewis, the artistic director, saw the staged reading and was impressed enough to invite me to join the ranks of Center Stage's associate artists. This was a turning point that led to my receiving, with Center Stage, a grant from the National Theatre Artist Residency Program, funded by the Pew Charitable Trusts and administered by Theatre Communications Group, providing the financial support to develop new plays in exchange for helping the theatre conceptualize new ways of including deaf theatre artists into their future productions.

Professional theatres should take the initiative to seek out long-term collaborations with deaf theatre artists. New artistic territories could be explored, particularly in visual and movement theatre. This would inevitably expand not only a theatre's subscription lists but also its artistic range.

To avoid ghettoization, even extinction, we should turn to our natural resources and devote more attention to nurturing the artistic growth of our deaf youth and students. We should do all we can to encourage high-profile hearing theatre artists to employ professional deaf theatre artists. If the media wants to review the work of deaf theatre artists, invite along a native informant, such as a theatre-savvy Deaf community liaison. The same should go for adjudicators or script readers. Most states have a Deaf association, a Deaf school, or a program with strong connections to the Deaf community. As more people see the potential for visual theatre and the capabilities of professional deaf theatre artists, then the minds in control of various theatre training institutions will also open up.

Eventually, a more sophisticated deaf and hearing audience will develop, which, in turn, will produce a stronger demand for quality signed or visual performances. Deaf theatre artists will need to assume more responsibility by aggressively seeking opportunities at their local professional theatres. These theatres should support deaf artists, knowing that it's beneficial for all in the long run. The internet can help because it is without communication barriers.

If all of this could be made to happen, deaf theatre and its artists would surely emerge from their invisible state into one that is invincible.

April 2001

Postscript to "From Lipreading Ants to Flying over Cuckoo Nests"

A lot has transpired in the realm of US Deaf theatres and Deaf theatre artists since I last wrote this article for *American Theatre* magazine twenty-one years ago. Established in 1991 under Deaf leadership, Deaf West Theatre is still going strong to this day. They have developed a phenomenal reputation and following, and have garnered worldwide recognition for their groundbreaking work in musical theatre on Broadway and in regional professional theatres. A good number of deaf actors who have trod the boards at Deaf West have gone on to do very notable stage, film, and TV work. The biggest and most recent accomplishment was made by one of Deaf West's longtime regulars, Troy Kotsur, who won a 2022 Academy Award for Best Supporting Actor in a feature film that also picked up an Oscar for Best Picture—*CODA*.

Deaf Spotlight, a nonprofit organization out of Seattle, Washington, that "showcases Deaf Culture and Sign Languages through the arts" since 2012, has grown beyond being the new kid on the block. They are now a force to reckon with by producing (of/by/for-the-Deaf) professional stage productions, film festivals, Deaf arts workshops, and events. Their vision is to "illuminate the artist within every deaf person."

New York Deaf Theatre (a small nonprofit established in 1979), who claims to be the third oldest Deaf theatre in America, has come into their own by producing professional productions in the greater New York City metro area. Their goal is to continue their mission of producing quality stage productions in ASL to both deaf and hearing audiences.

Over the past twenty years, Gallaudet University's theatre and dance program has allowed more and more theatre students to take ownership of their artistic creations on stage. Students are now writing more original scripts; developing their own set, lighting, costume, and sound designs; and auditioning for roles beyond Gallaudet's own productions. A wealth of creatives have emerged from the halls of Gallaudet University and made names for themselves in stage, TV, and film. Some of these names are Michelle Banks, Joey Caverly, Sandra Mae Frank, Tyrone Giordano, Russell Harvard, Amelia Hensley, Miranda Medugno, Lauren Ridloff, Warren "Wawa" Snipe, Jules Dameron, Shoshannah Stern, and Alexandria Wailes.

Leading the first wave of deaf professional designers is Ethan Sinnott, who has an MFA in scenic design, and Annie Wiegand with an MFA in lighting design. Both have been making inroads in their respective collaborations with various professional theatres around the United States. They are the inspiration for aspiring deaf students who wish to become designers or do professional work in technical theatre.

Unfortunately, deaf playwrights and directors still have not been able to make the same major advances in their careers as the above-mentioned theatre artists. Hopefully, as more professional deaf theatre artists become financially well off and can create job offers or establish funding for deaf playwrights and facilitate connections with their established industry networks on a national level in the so-called hearing entertainment world, then we will begin to see stories written and directed with an authentic deaf touch on stage, film, and TV.

June 5, 2022

Five Things a Visual Dramaturg Looks for That Might Surprise You

A visual dramaturg acts as the eyes of the deaf and hard of hearing audience. A visual dramaturg well versed in ASL and Deaf culture can be an invaluable consultant to a director, who may not know ASL and Deaf culture or may be just too busy to attend to this aspect of the production. My job during Gallaudet University's October 2014 main stage production of *Visible Language* has been to ensure that the overall stage presentation of sign language, open captioning, visual production elements, and Deaf culture-related matters are all on point with the script and clear to an audience.

There may be some overlap in the duties of the director of artistic sign language (DASL), depending on the depth and range of assigned responsibilities during a production. The DASL on *Visible Language* is Aaron Kubey, who has been heavily involved in the translation of the English dialogue and lyrics into ASL for the signing actors. He has also taught the ASL lines to actors who do not know signs.

Here are some of the production elements or visual concerns that I am always on the lookout for as a visual dramaturg:

1. **Are my eyes looking at the right places in the play?** A hearing audience's attention is drawn mostly by the direction of sounds or voices. A deaf audience's attention is guided by movement. A motion as simple as an actor unintentionally wiping his nose can draw the focus of the entire deaf audience away from something important happening on stage. Extraneous or intentional actor movement that inadvertently draws focus may need to be cut, rechoreographed, or timed differently. Sometimes this matter is resolved simply by getting the actor(s) to find ways to visually draw focus while the others nearby give focus where needed.

2. **Are signing sightlines clear for the deaf audience?** Spoken words can go through or around the body and reach the audience, but not signed words. Sometimes the signing of an

actor may get blocked by the positioning of certain actors (or props) on stage. Audience members sitting in the first couple of rows may not be able to see the hands of signers if there's an actor or two standing in the way.

3. **Are the captions well positioned and visible to the audience?** All of *Visible Language* will be captioned in plain view on a screen above the stage. I once dealt with a situation at a theatre that used projected captions. The very tip of the text was blocked by a set piece in front of the projector; none of the tech team noticed it until I mentioned it.

4. **Will the deaf audience understand name signs and locations that may seem out of context?** It is important to seek creative ways to introduce character names and places. Plays often have names of characters and locales. To the hearing ear, the English word lends itself to easy identification without any need for explanation. In Deaf culture, name signs are invented to represent a particular person. Take for example the name *Gallaudet.* It is created by forming the fingerspelled letter "G" and swinging it over one eye. This name sign came from the eyeglasses worn by Thomas Hopkins Gallaudet. It is also the name sign of the university where this play takes place. If the name *Gallaudet* comes up in dialogue, there has to be clear reference to what or who this name sign is in reference to: Thomas Gallaudet, his son Edward Miner Gallaudet, or the university itself. Inadvertent visual confusion must be avoided. For instance, the name sign for *Edward Miner Gallaudet* almost resembles the sign for *breasts*—so some kind of visual context needs to be created for the deaf audience to know that the dialogue topic at hand is not about breasts. Bottom line: Careful thought must go into ways to introduce character name signs and signs for locations to help the deaf audience with understanding exposition.

5. **Is the presentation of ASL legible on stage?** During the early part of the rehearsal process for *Visible Language,* the actor playing Helen Keller was exploring tactile reading of Annie Sullivan's signing. With historical accuracy, Helen was putting her hands over Annie's hands to "read" fingerspelled

and signed words. But from an audience's point of view, it was hard to understand what Annie was signing. The solution was to have Helen "cheat" a little by not covering so much of Annie's hands, and one way we found to do this was for the actor playing Helen to put her hands on the wrist of the actor playing Annie.

When you attend *Visible Language*, you may never notice everything that I as visual dramaturg must always be aware of and watch out for. But that's as it should be. If I've done my job right, you can just sit back enjoy the show!

About Willy Conley's background in visual dramaturgy:

My work as a visual dramaturg stems from watching the rehearsals of my fellow faculty directors, where we often ask each other for feedback on our respective productions. One of my early works in this capacity was at Center Stage in Baltimore during the production of The Hostage. *I was the associate director under Irene Lewis. In essence my role was really that of a visual dramaturg, since I was responsible for the direction and look of a signed song that was performed by the ensemble during the show. I have also worked a number of years as a DASL for various theatres such as Arena Stage, the Kennedy Center, Studio Theatre, and Everyman Theatre. It is my wish that more professional theatres involve the work of DASLs and visual dramaturgs when sign language is involved in future productions.*

October 2014

America Needs More Visual Theatre!

This was the headline used on a poster announcing a call for scripts written by deaf playwrights for the Visual Playwrights Retreat, produced over the past two summers by Quest: Arts for Everyone and Gallaudet University's Theatre Arts Department. The retreat offered deaf playwrights a rare opportunity either to enhance the visual elements of their scripts or to explore alternative ways to build scripts other than sitting alone writing in the traditional sense word by word in English, which is a second or third language for some. What prompted me to come up with the retreat slogan was that there had been way too much talking and very little physical movement going on in theatres nationwide. There seems to be a lot of actors in fantastic costumes standing around talking to each other for long periods of time on large stages with gorgeous sets. As I sat in various theatres—obviously a minority among hearing audience members—I thought: "These actors are getting away with wasting all of that space on stage with their almost holy ability to speak the English language to those who adore hearing it. Why isn't this play on the radio? Theatre should be a physical and visual medium."[1]

I understand that "talking-heads" theatre and musicals have their place in our society, but several of my deaf and hearing theatre colleagues and I feel that visual theatre deserves to have equal opportunity, funding, and recognition in the United States. Why not? Visual theatre is very popular in Europe, Asia, and the United Kingdom. According to the 2000 US Census, about twelve million Americans were linguistically isolated. That's up from 7.7 million in 1990, an increase of more than half. This indicates that more than ever American theatre companies need to vigorously explore ways to provide total theatre access to those who are linguistically isolated. An excellent way of

---

1. You may wonder what I was doing watching plays that were mostly verbal. Occasionally, I work as a sign master for ASL interpreters who are booked to sign interpret for a deaf audience during an evening or two at theatres in metro DC. Typically, sign masters coach and conduct rehearsals for interpreters by attending the same show four or five times.

providing access would be a visual, nonverbal production that would entertain any foreign language audience member. Good examples of visual theatre presenters are Cirque du Soleil, Blue Man Group, Bill Irwin, Mark Jaster, Robert Wilson, Pilobolus Dance Theatre, Squonk Opera, and Synetic Theatre.

So, what is visual theatre? A decent explanation of it is on the website of the School of Visual Theatre in Jerusalem, Israel (http://www.visualtheater.co.il/visual.html). Basically, it points out that the primary language of visual theatre is physical movement and/ or visual image; and that verbal language is secondary or nonexistent. One would find this form of theatre interdisciplinary, fusing various modes or elements of performance such as puppetry, circus arts, mime/gestures, multimedia, objects/props, lighting, sets, visual arts, masks, performance space, dance, sign language, audience participation, improvisation, music, and costumes.

Lyn Gardner, a theatre critic for *The Guardian*, wrote this on the website of the British Arts Council:

> . . . there is a strand of theatre—the physical and the visual—that speaks a completely different language from the traditional well-made play and spans theatre, puppetry, dance and visual arts. This work uses the language of gesture, an area of theatre that in the past was dubbed mime and thought of as entirely silent. Nowadays such pieces frequently include spoken text, but the body speaks as eloquently as the voice, and one of the great strengths of this form is that it can often mine the emotions that fall in the silences between words. Much of this work is devised not scripted . . . . (http://www.britishcouncil.org)

As part of the 2004 VSA arts festival at the Kennedy Center, I was a panelist for a roundtable discussion called "Access Deaf Theatre: Looking to the Future." We talked about the idea of creating an international visual theatre alliance or consortium, but nothing has been developed to date. Tim McCarty, president of Quest: Arts for Everyone, in Lanham, Maryland, has begun organizing a mini visual theatre consortium involving the MFA Intercultural-Interdisciplinary Theatre program at Towson University, The Theatre Project (in Baltimore), and Creative Alliance (also in Baltimore). The plan is to mount "Questfest" in 2006, a festival of visual theatre in Baltimore, to showcase the need for more visual theatre in our country. We are hoping that by starting out on a small scale, this may help spark interest leading to a larger visual theatre consortium someday that would eventually turn some of the bigger US theatre organizations on to incorporating some visual theatre into their seasons. For selfish reasons—being a Deaf theatre artist—I would like to see more opportunities created for folks like myself.

One day during the Visual Playwrights Retreat, we invited three influential Washington, DC, theatre artists who reviewed script submissions for their theatres. They were asked, "What would you do if you received a nontraditional or visual script of some type on a videotape, a CD, or a DVD? One of the artists replied that it would be a waste of his time. It would take too long to pop in a videotape and watch the work for one or two hours. Many of us were taken aback, since we all know that it usually takes at least an hour to sit down and read a full-length typewritten script. Why would sitting down to watch a videotape for an hour be much different? I would not be surprised if there were many other influential "gatekeepers" with similar attitudes in major theatres across the country. That was a signal to me that we have our work cut out for us.

March 2005

Hearing the Same Message

"It fell on deaf ears."
"He turned a deaf ear."
"Deaf as a post."
"Deaf and dumb."
"What's the matter, are you deaf?"
"I'm not deaf, I'm ignoring you."
"Stone deaf."
"Deafening applause."

How glibly these phrases are used by hearing people who have little awareness of the invisible population that coexists among them: those who are deaf and hard of hearing. How many realize that even though they have no land to claim as their own, deaf people have a rich and unique culture, language, and art that have shaped their identity? What contributions have they made to society? How about the light bulb . . . the telephone . . . the football huddle . . . baseball umpire signals . . . *Moonlight Sonata* . . . to name a few. With the rapid advances in medicine and technology that have led to cochlear implants, captioned TV and films, Telecommunication Devices for the Deaf, the internet, and genetic engineering, how much longer will the Deaf as a culture have before their identity gets aborted, deleted, or excised?

During my travels across America, I visited a few run-down, one-man Native American museums. I couldn't get it out of my mind that important artifacts and information from an oppressed culture were displayed in cheap, tactless ways. The cultures are not to blame, for society left them poor—emotionally, financially, and spiritually. With that in mind, I wrote the early drafts of *Falling on Hearing Eyes: A Museum of Sign/Anguish for People with Communication Disorders*.[1] I wanted to create a tragicomic visual gallery for the audience to tour from the comfort/discomfort of their seats.

---

1. Conley, *Vignettes*.

To demonstrate the various exhibits of the Deaf experience in this shabby touring show, I developed a couple of New Vaudevillian clowns, one deaf and one hearing. The deaf clown is the Guide and the hearing one is the Techie, the technician/sign language interpreter-in-training. No matter how hard the Guide communicates important information in literal and figurative sign language to the audience, the Techie manages to screw up the translation or the equipment that is supposed to help facilitate communication.

Most plays are written and directed for hearing actors and a hearing audience. Occasionally, these plays are interpreted in sign language for one night to a deaf audience. In some cases, a play is written and produced for deaf people and then translated in English for the hearing at every performance. One of my missions as a playwright is to create works that provide a total theatre experience for deaf and hearing audiences simultaneously. Another mission is to create roles for deaf actors that minimize the need for sign-interpreted shows, which tend to be tedious and an eyesore for deaf audience members.

As I further explore *Falling on Hearing Eyes* . . . during a two-week workshop at Center Stage in December with a creative team of actors, dramaturgs, and a director, I hope to find more provocative images that illuminate the complexities involved when deaf and hearing cultures merge.

1999

The Island of Intrigue

Fan Palm, infrared photograph

. . . Something about the Florida Keys that makes me wonder . . . was it a stumble into a transporter machine to patches of land stitched together by a worn-out thread of two-lane highway?

While palm trees bowed their heads in unison, billboards stood erect unaffected by the strength of the trade winds. Off in the distance, the surf softly applauded. "Key Lime Pie" is proudly advertised here and there, but an observant eye would detect the subtle fading of the lettering on the signs as the salt air takes its toll day by day (the locals claim that it ain't from the Keys if the pie is dyed green). Open air cafes speckle the highway's left and right shoulder, serving their customers a healthy shot of a breeze from the Keys.

At the southernmost tip of the United States lies the overlap of the Gulf of Mexico and the Atlantic. An idealist may expect to see a blurred line where the two bodies of water meet. A realist would see a zigzag line created by the tacking movements of a windsurfer slicing her way through the aqua-blue sea water. The line would soon be erased by the restless merge of the two seas.

It started to rain. A lone pelican of a mixed breed was struggling against the onrushing current. The rain matted the statue-gray feathers of the old shore bird to prevent it from escaping the rip tide. The windsurfer was nowhere to be seen.

On the sidewalk, behind the White Sands Restaurant, a street peddler was arranging a menagerie of conch shells. There were some with their natural colors, one that had been bleached white by the constant caressing of the sea, and others that were dyed pink.

Backtracking down the palm-lined street, sat the "Hemingway House" in its tropical environs. A heavyset woman was sitting in a metal folding chair next to the gateway. With a listless glare in her eyes, she mechanically collected the fare from tourists who wanted to see how Ernest arranged his furniture. A fluffy Persian strutted across the porch with an air of exasperation. The cat was waiting for the closing hour when the house would be free of pesky visitors, because he needed time to roam in and out of rooms to recollect old memories of rubbing his hind legs against the famous writer's short, stocky legs. The old Persian probably misses the coarse feeling of Ernest's salt-and-pepper beard against the smoothness of its musky fur. People say that Ernest had an affection for felines, and the six-toed ones from his time are still around, keeping his place pest free.

. . . there is an air of mystique about this island—a certain intriguing quality that a finger cannot place its print upon . . .

As I crossed the seven-mile bridge on the bus heading back toward the mainland of Florida, I turned around and watched the cluster of olive-green islands grow smaller and smaller amid the great pool of cyan. I muttered to the everwaving palm trees, "I shall be back."

February 1984

Watergraph

Watergraph was a term I invented that came from taking photographs of water reflections that have been turned upside-down. Depending on environmental factors like the wind, debris in the water, and the color of the sky, each inverted reflection created a painting in its own right framed by whatever was surrounding the water. This is part of my serendipitous quest for water reflections that range from little puddles to large bodies of water. You may want to turn the photo (or your head) upside-down to see how the image was originally discovered.

My favorite form of photography is "street shooting," which is simply going for random walks—wherever I am—with camera (or camera phone) in hand and recording anything that caught my eye. It was a technique I learned from one of my biomedical photography classes at the Rochester Institute of Technology where I was given an assignment called "Serendipity." I had to look up the word after class: an accidental discovery of things in a happy or beneficial way. At first, I was puzzled because everything I learned to photograph during my five years at college was planned and factual. I learned to relish the freedom to go out in the countryside, the water, the mountains, the city, the suburbs, even my own yard, and shoot anything that captivated me in the slightest way.

Deal Island House

Anchored at Harborplace

Little House on the Suburban Prairie

House in Savage

Boathouse, Westerly, RI

Spring 2011

Stages of Transformation
—*sidebar in Collaborations of the National Theatre Artist Residency Program*

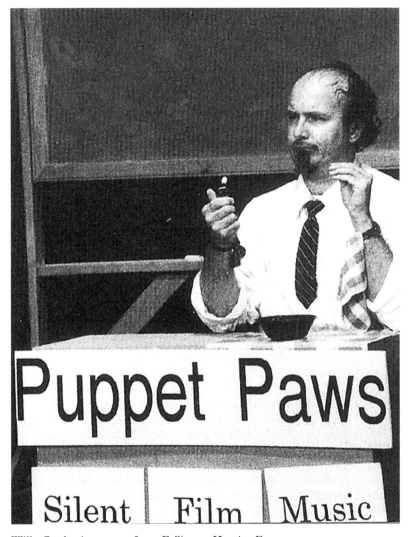

Willy Conley in a scene from *Falling on Hearing Eyes*

My residency [at Center Stage in Baltimore] made me realize that my plays come from a strong visual base. This makes my work difficult to appeal to a mainstream, literary-based hearing audience relying heavily on what is pleasing to the ear. If I want to appeal to a predominantly hearing audience, I would need to write plays that are literary and highly verbal. If I wrote such plays and they proved to be successful, I wonder if I would be personally satisfied knowing that people from my Deaf culture would probably neither see them nor have direct access to spoken language. I am still stubbornly exploring ways to bridge hearing and Deaf cultures in my plays, so that both types of audiences get a total theatre experience simultaneously.

2005

Warm and Inspiring
—*sidebar to the NTID Focus article*, "Portraits of Success"

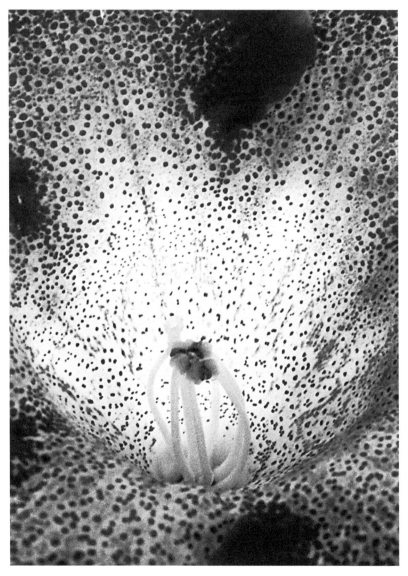

Orchid

"Gallery Row," along La Cienega Boulevard near Melrose, provided the perfect backdrop against which to display the paintings, photographs, and furniture that comprised "Heart/Eye/Hand."

At twilight on May 27, 1986, the doors of the Ankrum Gallery opened to a waiting crowd. It was a pleasantly warm evening, with the scent of jasmine in the air. A short trail of taillights streaked by as the procession of cars along the Boulevard became less frequent. It was the ebbing of L.A.'s rush hour.

The opening piece in the gallery was a simple yet beautiful oil painting of a vacant chair in the corner of the room. In that room was an open window overlooking several rooftops. The scene seemed rather symbolic since, in the past, creative works of deaf artists have been somewhat inaccessible to the public. Finally, the opportunity for access had been opened.

Through the doors walked sharply dressed people, young and old, from as far away as New York to as near as neighboring communities. Actors, artists, businesspeople, interpreters, photographers, teachers, and writers mingled. Some were regular gallery "goers"; others had never attended an exhibit opening.

Refreshments were served as guests strolled about, viewing the art along the perimeters of the gallery. At times they sat on benches to study a particular piece.

Many guests wanted to meet the artists, and approached them with compliments, questions, criticisms, and even purchase offers. The atmosphere provoked discussion, piqued curiosity, and commanded respect.

Hugs, smiles, and laughter were exchanged while an occasional flashbulb captured these moments. It was a reunion of sorts, with old friendships renewed and new ones created.

Passersby looking through the window could see a montage—stationary art among an array of fluid hands, facial expressions, and body movements drawing their own forms of art.

As I left the gallery, I thought, "This cultural event was desperately needed. It should happen wherever a Deaf community exists."

"Heart/Eye/Hand" was warm and inspiring, visually stimulating, and done with touch.

Fall 1986

Bicyclists Welcome

Basel Bike

During a visit to Basel, Switzerland, I wandered up the road along the Rhine River, taking in the region known for being the center of the humanist movement. Seeing this bike on an old road near the medieval-looking door conjured up Old World simplicity. Later, I read a travel brochure on Basel that said cyclists would feel at home "in this bike-friendly town."

March 2002

Mushrooms

They say that mushrooms and fungi are resilient organisms, highly resistant to stress. They have a fleshy resistance and can sprout overnight. They are practically everywhere yet easy to overlook. Merlin Sheldrake once wrote: "They are humble yet astonishingly versatile organisms, eating rock, making soil, digesting pollutants, nourishing and killing plants, surviving in space, inducing visions, producing food, making medicines, manipulating animal behavior, and influencing the composition of the earth's atmosphere."[1]

Mushroomrise

---

1. Martin Sheldrake, *Entangled Life: How Fungi Make Our Worlds, Change Our Minds and Shape Our Futures* (New York: Random House, 2020).

Childrearing

Pine Needle Umbrella

The Rolodex Mushroom

Inside the Mind of a Mushroom

Spring 2021

The Loneliest Game in the World

There is a young boy in my neighborhood who plays baseball by himself every day almost all year round. His diamond is in a lot next to the mailboxes for our townhome community. You can tell he plays there often because the four corners of the diamond, where the bases should be, have worn spots in the grass. He's the only one seen playing the imaginary game before thousands of imaginary fans.

He's always in full uniform wearing the number 8 with the name "Ripken" above it, in honor of his hero Cal of the Baltimore Orioles. All pitching, catching, hitting, base running, and umpiring are performed by the little Ripken wannabe. He wears a hearing aid behind his right ear and always cocks his head slightly to one side. With thick eyeglasses and a tilted view of the world, he seems to be in perpetual confusion.

He is never seen with a father or an older male. His big brothers and sisters play around him or beyond him but never with him. Once in a while, his mother with an everpresent cigarette in her mouth takes him somewhere in a van. If she and I happen to open our mailboxes at the same time, she never acknowledges my presence although I'm always ready for eye contact, to wave a hello or nod my head with a smile. She is very pale and thin, has a four-leaf clover tattoo on the side of her neck, and is often seen with different men visiting her at night.

I caught a glimpse of her one morning waving the "I-Love-You" sign to her son as he rode away on the back of a school bus with no one else inside except the driver. It was the only time I saw any communication between the boy and his mother.

One day I was walking to the community mailboxes and saw him sitting on his front porch, head hanging in his hands, as he gazed down at the sidewalk. A baseball helmet, glove, and an aluminum bat were sprawled out in the grass nearby. As if suddenly called from the dugout, he slowly got up like an aging ballplayer and put on his helmet. He trotted out to first base and went into a runner's crouch, wary of a pick-off from the mound.

As I opened my mailbox, I watched him out of the corner of my eye. He ran to second base and slid into it. He lay there for a minute. I was hesitant about whether to go out there to see if he was all right or not. I decided against it; I had never gotten the nerve or the opportunity to introduce myself to him before and to do it then with him lying in the grass was a bit too weird. Groggily, he got up and brushed the dirt off his pants. Assuming the umpire's position, he gestured, "Safe!"

Yes, I thought, he's safe for another day but for how much longer? A young deaf boy can only fall and get back up by himself for so long before he'll remain fallen, forever injured in the baseball game of life.

Summer 2001

The Psychic Cat Vendor

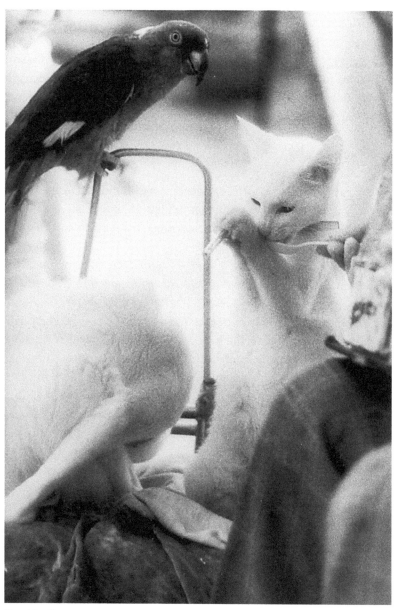

Psychic Cat

There's a man who comes to the La Brea Tar Pits every day wearing a tie, a ski cap pulled down to his ears, and an overcoat with bird droppings down his back. His routine is to tote a rusted luggage cart and a cage covered in black cloth over to one of the palm trees surrounding the Lake Pit. A stench of rotten eggs permeates the April air, not from the man but from hydrogen sulfide burping up to the surface of the pit where a statue of a gray mastodon stuck in tar extends its massive trunk and tusks skyward in a frozen snarl. On the man's shoulder is a parrot, and once the man sets everything down, the parrot jumps over to the cart handle and paces side to side, squawking at passersby like a robust circus barker. Usually by then, a small, hesitant gathering of adults and children draw forth. The parents keep their arms over their children like seat belts.

The man doesn't talk. His dark eyes sweep rapidly back and forth over the bystanders in contradiction to his slow and deliberate movements. Meanwhile, he unties old shoestrings that hold down a wooden box with a bird sculpted on top of it.

The man places a cracked mirror against the side of the tree. Colored rhinestones are glued to its surface, arranged in crooked lettering: "TRAINED PETS GIVE GOOD LUCK." Next, the black cloth is whipped off the wire cage revealing two albino cats. Their tails snake in and out between the bars with a slither that beckons people to come closer. The man pulls out a can of cat food from his coat pocket and opens it with a dime store can opener. He feeds the cats little morsels from a spoon.

On the ground with his back against the tree trunk, the man puts the wooden bird box on his lap. He whispers to the sparrow and gives it a gentle pat on the head. He takes out one of the cats and scoops up a small chunk of food, waving it teasingly in front of the cat's nose. The cat swipes and misses.

The man holds the spoon closer to the sparrow. Another swipe and miss, but this time the cat strikes the bird's tail, thus tilting it backward. A small cellophane tube rolls out of the bottom of the box. The parrot quickly retrieves it with its talons and flies back to its perch. The man rewards the cat with a generous lump of cat chow.

The man motions to a young girl from the crowd to come and take the tube. The parrot transfers the tube to its beak. The girl, not wanting to risk getting too close, reaches out as far as she can and grasps the tube with two fingers. She runs back to her mother who slips off the plastic wrapping to read its contents. The dirty, smudged message with an ornamental border of harps and cherubs reads:

> ajust your rhithim to thosc around. come out difficalt cycul to good job, money, love, and family together. i love you deeply
> —Psychic Cat

The man picks up the other cat and tricks it into hitting the bird tail lever. Another message pops out. A young boy volunteers to take it from the parrot. His father hands him a quarter to give to the man, which starts the man's trickle of income for the day. Meanwhile, the mother takes the message from her daughter, glances around to make sure no one's looking, and drops the fortune slip on the ground behind her as they leave. Other people come forward for a prediction of their future and throw a few coins on the ground. They hang around and wait, expecting the unexpected, but eventually they get bored and leave.

The man tucks the cats back into the cage and lifts the parrot onto his shoulder. He scrapes up his coins and drops them into his coat pocket. He walks over to where the crowd stood and goes down on his knees to pick up the littered psychic messages. He brushes the dirt off the papers, rolls them back up and slides them into their cellophane tubes again. The last one he furls up says:

> new area solution of conflict in your faver. period of learning something new.strong money lots. break thru for you with eksellent situation.so good luck in new faze in life. i love you deeply
> —Wizard Cat

Piling all of the little scrolls together, he drops them through a slot behind the wooden box and then straps it back onto the luggage cart.

After he covers the cage with black cloth, he picks it up and hobbles over to the other side of the pit to find another tree to set up his next performance. The parrot on his shoulder jerks his head every which way, and the cats in the dark meow loudly, not knowing where they're going. A pigeon flies in and squats on the mammoth's back while tar bubbles release oily film on the pit's surface near the statue's legs—all oblivious to the expression of rage on the mastodon's face.

2022

PLAYLETS: NONVERBALS

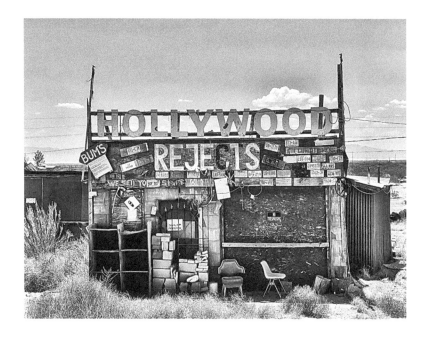

The Deaf Chef
—a comical cook-off

Note: All of the actors in this piece must be deaf and pretend to be hearing. The entire piece has the feel, look, and pace of a silent film. Silent film, Three Stooges, and Looney Tunes music should underscore various aspects of this play. When the DEAF CHEF enters, something dramatic, like Mozart's Eine Kleine Nachtmusik, *plays.*

Setting: a long, sturdy table; nearby on an easel is a large picture of a pizza pie and the words: INTERNATIONAL PIZZA COOK-OFF.

A prim and proper male culinary judge enters with enthusiasm and mouths silently to the audience his introduction to the cook-off. He invites the international female contestants onstage and introduces each one. They wear chef hats and their country's flag on their smocks. Each says her name and a few words about where she's from, and sends a flirtatious signal to the judge as a way to win him over.

Undaunted for the most part, the judge reads off the last name on the list. Everyone looks in the direction of where the last contestant should be, but she turns out to be a no-show. The judge leads the women to their spots behind the table and indicates a lump of dough ready for each of them. He briefly goes over the rules, using his clipboard and showing his bell that he will ring if any of them get disqualified.

On the count of three, he gestures for them to get on their mark, get ready, and go. On "ready," one contestant jumps the gun by going ahead to prepare the dough. He orders her back. He goes through the counting motions again and off they go in a rapid action sequence, each showing off their distinctive pizza cooking techniques.

The judge pulls out a large magnifying glass, cleans it, and holds it behind his back. He walks by each one, on the alert for any rule-breakers. When he suspects one is about to break a rule, he pulls the glass out and watches closely. When this happens, the contestant goes into slow motion and breaks a rule while the others are frozen in action. Ideas for breaking the rules could be things like sneezing onto the pizza, having a hair fall into the food, lighting a cigarette, cutting a finger and trying to stop the bleeding, dropping a pizza topping on the floor and putting it back on the pie, whatever . . . . When a rule gets broken, the judge hits his little bell and disqualifies the contestant. He gestures quickly to indicate which rule was broken.

As more and more contestants become disqualified, they stand in line off to the side and watch the others to see who is going to win. It ends up that all of them get disqualified. Disappointed, the judge takes his arm and wipes all of the ingredients off the table and onto the floor.

From offstage enters the DEAF CHEF. There should be something physically different about her. She could be diminutive, tall, large, or of a different skin color. Something must stand out over the rest of them. The contestants mouth words to each other about the latecomer. The DEAF CHEF taps on the judge's shoulders and signs quickly and elaborately, apologizing for her lateness. The judge is confused by this flurry of hand activity. She gestures clearly that she is deaf. The judge reacts nonverbally: "Oh! You're deaf!" And then pitifully: "Awwww . . . I'm so sorry!!!" She begs him to let her cook her recipe. He gives in.

Up to the count of three, she does some warm-ups. The DEAF CHEF has highly unorthodox food preparation techniques like jumping up on the table and stomping on the dough to spread it out, karate-chopping vegetables, sawing pepperoni, hammering some toppings to a pulp, and so on. Each topping gets put on the pizza in visual and unusual ways. Incredible as it may seem, none of the cooking rules have been broken despite the judge's attempt to find one among his pages of rules.

Meanwhile, the other contestants and the judge are absolutely flabbergasted. With every cooking technique that the DEAF CHEF uses, there are silent reactions from the others.

Finally, after having thrown the pizza in the oven and then taken it out in compressed cartoon time, the DEAF CHEF slices the pie with flair and offers the judge a piece. She closes her eyes in nervousness and hope.

The judge takes the slice reluctantly and tastes it. He chews on it a while with no reaction. Then we see his facial and body expressions slowly show signs of ecstasy. He faints from swallowing the most exquisite, scrumptious, delicious slice of pizza he's ever had.

Others become curious and crowd in on him. One of them takes the slice out of his hands and tastes it. She shows signs of extreme pleasure. At the next bite, they all close in, taking a bite at the same time, accidentally kissing one another in the process.

No longer able to keep her eyes closed, the DEAF CHEF opens them and looks at the scene before her. She sees the judge out cold on the floor and the others behaving very strangely.

She goes to the table upset, picks up the rest of her pie, and dumps it on the ground. In slow motion, the contestants gesture for her not to do that. They all make a mad slo-mo scramble for the discarded slices on the floor. The DEAF CHEF packs up her imaginary cooking tools and walks away. She stops and looks back, seeing everyone on the floor gobbling up pizza like pigs. She shakes her head, shrugs, and exits. The contestants, converting to normal action speed, get up, point toward the DEAF CHEF, and run offstage in her direction.

The judge awakens and vaguely remembers he tasted something extraordinary on his lips. He looks around and recalls the DEAF CHEF and her exotic recipe. He gestures to the audience, indicating an obvious physical description of her, asking where she went. He mouths some words and holds his hand over his heart to show his love for her. He senses the direction she went and dashes offstage. The end.

2009

Remains of Bosnians
—a monodrama

Note: It is important that the audience be arranged at a level higher than the stage. It makes no difference whether the janitor is male or female.

An empty room except for a bone-white strip of carpeting the size of a coffin. Beside one end of the carpet is a clay pot of soil with a small dead plant or tree about three to four feet in height.

A janitor in blue coveralls enters the room whistling, holding in one hand a red portable Dirt Devil vacuum cleaner and a broom. The janitor whistles tunelessly and is very casual throughout this whole piece. In the other hand, the janitor carries or pushes/pulls a small cart of various household cleaners and pesticides—Ty-D-Bowl, Lysol, Fantastik, ammonia, roach killer, wasp killer, etc. A bag of potting soil is also in the cart.

The janitor puts everything down and goes over to inspect the carpet.

The janitor picks up a can of roach killer and sprays the air around and above the carpet. The audience should be able to pick up the scent.

Satisfied, the janitor goes over to the plant and sticks a finger into the soil.

The janitor brings the bag of soil and an empty jar over to the plant. The janitor picks up a handful of soil and sifts it back into the bag, watching the dirt fall. With the jar, the janitor scoops out dirt and pours it into the pot.

The janitor gets out the toilet bowl cleaner and squeezes a good amount of blue fluid into the freshly added soil.

The janitor scoops another jarful of dirt, goes over to the carpet, kneels before it and sprinkles out the following letters using the dirt: REMAINS OF BOSNIANS.

The janitor stands up and backs away a little to take in the words from a wider perspective. The janitor stops whistling and becomes serious. The janitor looks up toward the ceiling. After looking for about twenty to thirty seconds and seeing nothing happen, the janitor resumes whistling with casual demeanor.

The Dirt Devil gets plugged in and the janitor vacuums up the lettered dirt from the carpet.

The janitor unplugs the vacuum cord and winds it up and puts it down.

The janitor gets the broom and sweeps up the dirt on the floor that was blown off the carpet. The janitor builds up a little pile beside the carpet, lifts the carpet, sweeps the pile under it, and then lays the carpet back down.

The janitor carries the cart, the broom, and the vacuum cleaner and leaves the room, still whistling.

Lights fade to black.

December 1995

The Practice of Medicine
—a performance art monodrama

At preset, a light reveals a yellowish-white, old-fashioned one-door refrigerator at center stage. A piece of yellow police tape—with the word CAUTION written across it—is taped to stage right side of the refrigerator and extended at an angle toward downstage right about ten feet to a metal pole (the kind used for creating velvet-rope barriers in movie theatres). The tape is wrapped around this pole and extended across to another pole toward downstage left and gets wrapped around that. The tape ends up back on the refrigerator to its stage left side area to look like a taped-off crime scene. Outside of this area, a TV monitor is set to the left or right.

Inside the taped-off area and about three feet in front of the refrigerator is a dinette table and chair. On the table is a box of Cheerios, a banana, a yellow bowl, a spoon, and the Sunday comics.

Lights go down. On the upper half of the refrigerator door, a projected title slide in simple black lettering on white background fades up: "The Practice of Medicine." A video fades up revealing an opera singer singing an aria from *Madama Butterfly* in a foreign language with English subtitles.

Another light shows a man dressed in a bathrobe and slippers, sitting at the table pouring Cheerios into the bowl. He gets up and takes out a carton of milk from the lit but otherwise empty refrigerator.

After he closes the door and sits down, the next slide comes up.

Slide (image): A surgeon at the operating table.

Each subsequent slide should be projected every eight to ten seconds until the end.

The man slices the banana into his cereal.

Slide (text): ADVANCED

He pours milk.

Slide (image): An infant hooked up to intravenous tubes and monitors.

From here until the end the man eats his cereal unemotionally while reading the comics.

Slide (text): FUN!

Slide (image): Deformed lab rat with forceps squeezing a tumor on it.

Slide (text): HOT AND FRESH

Slide (image): Close-up of a tiny red premature baby, with a hand holding a stethoscope on the baby.

Slide (text): CLEAN

Slide (image): A bloodied hand with an amputated finger.

Slide (text): ALL NATURAL

Slide (image): A three-quarter shot of a patient facing away from the camera; an arm is missing.

Slide (text): FEAST FOR TASTE BUDS

Slide (image): Close-up shot of a patient's mouth with lips held back to show cancerous lesions on the gums and inside of mouth.

Slide (text): BIGGER AND BETTER

Slide (image): Surgical photo of a volleyball-sized abdominal tumor; a gloved hand rests over it.

Slide (text): JUST PERFECT

Slide (image): A headshot of a patient with nose and mouth gone; the two sides of the face have been sewn together.

Slide (text): 99% FAT FREE

Slide (image): Pathology photo of a colon cut open revealing a gumball-sized tumor.

Slide (text): HOMEMADE GOODNESS

Slide (image): Close-up surgical shot of gloved fingers holding an ovarian cyst.

Slide (text): CRISPY

Slide (image): A medium shot of third-degree burns on a patient's legs.

Slide (text): EASY

Slide (image): Close-up of the underside of a wounded penis; a hypodermic needle has penetrated the skin.

Slide (text): SMELLS GREAT

Slide (image): Shot of a patient's buttocks showing bedsores and bone.

Slide (text): REFRESHING

Slide (image): Shot of venereal warts in a patient's vaginal area.

Slide (text): SENSATIONAL

Slide (image): Shot of conjoined twins.

Slide (text): GUARANTEED

Slide (image): Full-body shot of a patient's back that shows blisters that have broken open.

Slide (text): INSTANT RELIEF

Slide (image): Autopsy photo of a brain being removed from a corpse's head.

The man picks up the bowl slurps down what's left of the bowl. The aria comes to an end.

Slide (text; all the words should squeeze into the frame): PIGMENTARY GLAUCOMA DOUBLE-BARREL COLOSTOMY EXPLORATORY LAPAROTOMY AMBIGUOUS GENITALIA SILICONE BUCKLE RHYTIDECTOMY DIVERTICULITIS RHINOPLASTY BLEPHAROPLASTY

Lights fade to black.

December 1995

Disconnected
—a monodrama

Darkness. A column of light comes up on a rotary telephone on a stand. Another light illuminates the long telephone cord that's plugged into a wall jack.

A haggard deaf character, around fifty years old, comes into the light and stares at the phone for a long time.

In a hesitant manner, the character picks up the receiver and looks at it from all angles. The character presses the hang-up buttons on the cradle of the base unit a few times.

The character dials a seven-digit number and looks at the receiver. No response.

The character looks at the base unit. No response.

The character waves a hand in front of the receiver. No response.

With one hand the character signs something incomprehensible to one end of the receiver. No response. The character tries the other end. No response.

The character looks closely into the holes of both ends of the receiver. Nothing. The character lays the receiver down, backs up, and with two hands signs something desperately and incomprehensibly to the receiver. No response. The character acts increasingly desperate.

The character picks up the receiver and unscrews one end to look inside. Electronic parts dangle from it. The character does the same to the other end. More parts hang or fall out. The character looks inside the handle. Nothing.

The character fingers the cord that connects the receiver to the base unit. The character unplugs the cord from the receiver end and drops the receiver on the floor. The character signs something incomprehensible to the cord end. No response.

The character looks at it up close. When the character sees nothing, the character traces the cord down to where it's connected to the side of the base unit and unplugs it there. The character throws the receiver cord away and tries to look inside the base unit where the cord was plugged. Nothing.

The character signs something incomprehensible to the base unit jack. No response.

The character picks up the unit and looks at it from all angles. Nothing.

The character unplugs the wall cord that's connected to the back of the unit and drops the unit.

The character look at the end of the wall plug. Nothing.

The character signs something incomprehensible to the cord end. No response.

The character follows the cord down to the wall jack and unplugs it. The character gets down to the floor and eyeballs the jack. Nothing. The character backs up a little and signs something incomprehensible to it. No response.

The character tries to stick fingers into the jack, to remove it, but can't. Breathing becomes heavy.

The character turns back to the jack and slumps against the wall.

As the breathing goes down, so do the lights.

Darkness.

The End

January 1998

The Fire Place
—a short screenplay

Fade in:

EXT. HOUSE #1—DAY
It is a windy, sunny late fall afternoon on a prairie, a farm, or someplace in the middle of nowhere. We see a lone, simple one-story house with an old, barren tree in the yard with branches almost touching the house. A car with New York plates is parked nearby. A "for sale" sign with the word "SOLD" across it leans against the wall of the house.

INT. HOUSE #2—DAY
In the sparse house among scattered U-Haul boxes, a dog is asleep on a rug by a pair of crossed legs in pajama pants with feet in slippers.

On top of an upright suitcase is a lone goldfish in a goldfish bowl with a miniature fireplace ornament in it, as if she has her own human-like home. Each living thing in the house is in its own world—the man, the dog, and the fish.

Sunlight sparkles in the goldfish water. The sun shines through and casts a shadow of the window on the floor next to the dog. Shadows of leaves and branches sway in the wind.

The dog's ears twitch in response to the creaking of the tree outside, the scratching of its branches against the house. Without moving his head, the dog's eyes open and look up at its owner.

The fish is looking in the direction of its owner.

From the slippers the camera pans up the pajama legs to reveal someone reading the *Silent News*, *Deaf Nation*, or some newspaper by deaf individuals. Every now and then, a page turns but we do not see the face yet.

All of a sudden there is a loud thump. The dog yelps and jumps away, frightened, whimpering. A can of fish food rolls off the suitcase and lands on the floor. Fish food flakes spill out.

The fish is darting back and forth rapidly in the bowl.

Another page of newspaper is turned over. The top part of a page is folded back by the new homeowner, and we see his world-weary eyes. He has a face that has seen enough bullshit in the world to escape to this place of solitude. His eyes roam around the room in reaction to a change in the air. He notices the dog is no longer at his feet. He looks at the goldfish and sees she is swimming a high-speed marathon in circles.

He puts down the deaf news and picks up the *New York Times* newspaper and goes back to his reading.

The dog scampers back and sniffs the spilled fish food. He licks up a few flakes, likes it, and laps the rest on the floor. The fish stops, hovers in the water and looks in the direction of the dog.

The man notices that the light coming in the room somehow looks different. He gets up to look out the window but doesn't see anything. Then, he goes to the door. The door bumps into something outside.

EXT. HOUSE FRONT #3—DAY

The tree, which fell over, is either leaning against the door or has a large branch blocking it. The man pushes against the door to widen it, but can only open it a few inches to get his arm out. The dog sticks his nose out, but he can't get out either.

INT. HOUSE #4—DAY

The man gets a handsaw out of a box. He goes out the back kitchen door. The dog follows him. The fish watches them leave.

EXT. HOUSE FRONT #5—DAY

The man comes around the house and saws the first piece of the tree away from the front door. The following could be a montage or a sped-up action sequence. He saws some more, painstakingly stacking up the pieces as they're cut. Every now and then he throws a stick for the dog to chase. He cuts the tree down to its last log and branch.

EXT. HOUSE SIDE #6—EVENING

By early evening, the side of the house has a neatly stacked woodpile with branches. He is very pleased with his work. The dog is content with a stick in his mouth.

INT. HOUSE #7—EVENING

The man enters, along with the dog, and turns on a light. The fish is calm in the water. The man pats the dog in thanks for the support of keeping him company. He throws him a treat.

The man notices the opened fish food canister on the floor. He sees that there is no fish food anywhere. He looks at the dog. The dog looks away, settles on the floor, and licks his paws.

Hovering in front of his little fireplace, the fish looks at the man.

The man goes to the kitchen cupboard. Bare. He opens the refrigerator. A carton of milk and a loaf of white bread sit on the top shelf. He takes out a slice of bread and crumples a few tiny pieces into the goldfish bowl. The fish nibbles at it hungrily. The man nibbles at the rest of the bread slice. He shivers.

EXT. HOUSE SIDE #8—EVENING

The man goes outside to load a few logs and sticks onto his arms, and carries them inside the house.

INT. DEN #9—EVENING

He looks along his four walls, and it slowly dawns on him that his new house doesn't have a fireplace.

The fish calmly hovers in the water and looks at the man. The dog looks up at the man. The man stands there unsure of what to do.

He decides to go out the kitchen door to the backyard.

EXT. HOUSE BACK #10—EVENING

He sets up the wood and sticks in tepee style, and begins a fire. He sits on the back steps. The dog gets up and joins him. They watch the fire for a little bit.

The man goes back in the house and returns with the goldfish bowl. He sets it on the steps where all three can watch the fire. He leans over and looks through the bowl at eye level with the goldfish. He points to the little fireplace in the bowl and gestures "thumbs up" to the fish.

The dog looks at him, cocks his head quizzically, and barks. The three continue to watch the fire.

Fade out.

The End

June 2021

PLAYLETS: VERBALS

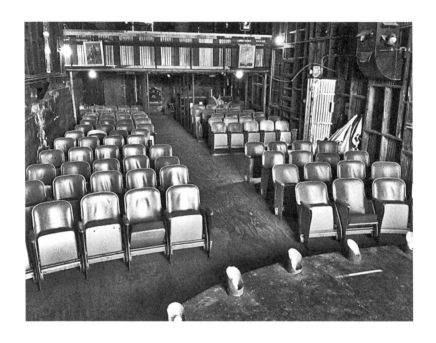

Dialogue of the Deaf
—a cultural sightbite

Setting: Nail salon in a strip mall; the present.

Lights go up on two deaf women conversing in ASL while getting a pedicure. Their pedicurists are hearing but invisible to the audience; they do not know ASL.

DEAF WOMAN A: Hey-hey-hey—not that color. I told you Bahamian Blue. Fucking idiot can't understand me.

(Exaggerates lip movements: "blue, blue, blue"; gestures to the color of her blouse—blue.) Same on my toe. Fuckin' hearing people—can't even understand a simple pointing gesture. And they call us "deaf and dumb." Right?

DEAF WOMAN B: Look—you shouldn't be saying that.

DEAF WOMAN A: She can't understand me, what're you worried about?

DEAF WOMAN B: Your attitude—body language. I'm sure she gets it.

DEAF WOMAN A: She ain't getting the Bahamian Blue, that's for sure! Lemme ask you something—if a deaf person has to go to court, is it still called a hearing?

DEAF WOMAN B: I don't know what you're talking about.

DEAF WOMAN A: You know how people go to court for a hearing? Well, if deaf people go, what do we call it?

DEAF WOMAN B: I don't know.

DEAF WOMAN A: Exactly my point! We shouldn't call it a "hearing" though, right?

DEAF WOMAN B: Hmmm, I guess not . . .

DEAF WOMAN A: And do you ever read—*(to pedicurist)* OW! Easy— you went too deep. (*gestures "take it easy"*) You think she did that on purpose??

DEAF WOMAN B: I don't know, maybe it was a little accident.

DEAF WOMAN A: Anyway, you ever read in newspapers headlines like "Dialogue of the Deaf?"

DEAF WOMAN B: No, I don't think so. What's that?

DEAF WOMAN A: I see it all the time. Why do fuckin' hearing people keep saying that? It makes no sense. You and I can dialogue all day long till the cows come home. And I'm so sick of this one: "Fall on deaf ears." You ever seen that phrase?

DEAF WOMAN B: Never.

DEAF WOMAN A: Hearing people write that all the time in newspapers and magazines. I'm gonna start saying, "It fell on hearing eyes."

DEAF WOMAN B: Sorry, I'm totally lost.

DEAF WOMAN A: Instead of information not coming through the ears, it will hit the eyes and bounce off. Like hearing can't see or comprehend anything. Know what I mean?

DEAF WOMAN B: Aahhh!

DEAF WOMAN A: So, you get it?

DEAF WOMAN B: No, but this feels wonderful. My pedicurist is really good.

Lights down fast.

Spring 2021

Naturalization
—a short farce

Note: Since this is a play about an immigrant applying for US citizenship, the role of FELICIA may be interchangeable according to the current political climate and/or the availability, ethnicity, and gender of deaf actors. Character name and affected lines may be revised to match the above information exchange.

Characters:

FELICIA MARIA DELGADO, deaf female applicant from Mexico; actor should be reasonably fluent in ASL.

INTERPRETER, sign language interpreter intern; hearing, male; actor should be fluent in ASL and able to Sim-Com effectively (while needing to come across authentically as an intern).

OFFICER SWALLOW, immigration services clerk; hearing, male.

Time: Present.
Setting: US Citizenship and Immigration Services in Los Angeles; interview office with waiting area; a large portrait of the current US president is in the background, overseeing the action.

As lights come up, FELICIA is sitting in the waiting area reading a magazine. OFFICER SWALLOW is doing mundane paper-pushing chores at his desk: stamping forms, shuffling papers, sharpening pencils, organizing paper clips, etc.

INTERPRETER enters, looks among the others in the waiting room, and stands fairly close to FELICIA, who is seated and engrossed in her magazine. He signs and speaks throughout the play except where noted.

INTERPRETER: *(voices to the applicants in the room)* I'm the sign language interpreter for someone named . . . Felicia Maria Delgado? I'm not sure of the spelling but . . .

Realizes his mistake, and repeats the above in signs.

Uh, sorry to interrupt your . . . your wait.

OFFICER SWALLOW finishes his little desk chores.

OFFICER SWALLOW: Number 352. 3-5-2.

(no response)

352?

INTERPRETER: Excuse me, are you Felicia?

(FELICIA nods her head.)

INTERPRETER: Is your number 352?

(She nods.)

(to OFFICER SWALLOW)

Uh, sir, we're 352. I'm interpreting for a client who cannot hear.

FELICIA: Where's Sheila Barton *(sign name S.B. on the chest)*?

INTERPRETER: Sheila Barton *(S.B.)* called in sick today.

FELICIA: I've never met you before.

INTERPRETER: That's right, we've never met. I'm a new interpreting intern.

FELICIA: You're an intern?? Why didn't I get certified interpreter?

INTERPRETER: I'm sorry. No other certified interpreters were available at the last minute.

FELICIA: Oh my god! My green card will soon expire—I must pass my US citizenship interview.

INTERPRETER: I understand, you must pass your citizenship interview. Calm down—I promise I will do my best. *(pause)* My boss told me to ask: Do you prefer ASL, ORAL, PSE, SEE I, SEE II, LOVE, SIM-COM, Total Communication, the Rochester Method, International Sign, Gestures, or Cued Speech?

FELICIA: *(long pause)* ASL, please.

OFFICER SWALLOW: 352! I don't have all day.

(INTERPRETER lets FELICIA know she's being called in. During the interview, the interpreter translates in sign language what OFFICER SWALLOW says. The interpreter also voice interprets what FELICIA signs.)

OFFICER SWALLOW: My name is Officer Swallow; badge number 451.

(INTERPRETER signs "He what? Police swallow 451.")

OFFICER SWALLOW: Please come in. *(pause)* Why is she backing away?

INTERPRETER: I don't know.

FELICIA: He swallowed a cop??

OFFICER SWALLOW: What did she say?

INTERPRETER: She wanted to clarify your name. *(to FELICIA)* No, no—his name: Officer S-w-a-l-l-o-w.

OFFICER SWALLOW: *(showing name tag)* Tell her—me Swallow—like a bird.

INTERPRETER signs: He S-w-a-l-l-o-w, Bird.

OFFICER SWALLOW: She looks very nervous—is she okay?

INTERPRETER: You okay?

(FELICIA shakes her head: "No.")

OFFICER SWALLOW: Nervous is normal. Tell her that before we begin the interview, I need to place her under oath. Please raise your right hand.

(INTERPRETER interprets, and raises his left hand. FELICIA raises her left hand.)

OFFICER SWALLOW: Her hand—not yours!

INTERPRETER: Sorry! (*to FELICIA*) Other hand . . .

FELICIA switches to her right hand.

OFFICER SWALLOW: *(automatic and fast)* Doyouswearoraffirmthatthestatementsyouwillgivetodaywillbethetruththewholetruthandnothingbutthetruth?

INTERPRETER: I got as far as swear.

FELICIA: I'm lost.

OFFICER SWALLOW: Doyouswearoraffirmthatthestatementsyouwillgivetodaywillbethetruththewholetruthandnothingbutthetruth?

INTERPRETER: Do you swear something-something-xwrxobyezthsbsltybllrrr . . . truth? Just say "I do."

FELICIA: I do what?

INTERPRETER: Just say yes.

FELICIA: Yes.

INTERPRETER: *(voices only)* I do.

OFFICER SWALLOW: You do or she do?

INTERPRETER: She.

OFFICER SWALLOW: Very well.

He looks at FELICIA's application or at the INTERPRETER during this inquiry.

Passport, please.

FELICIA hands over her passport to INTERPRETER. INTERPRETER gestures "no," give it to OFFICER SWALLOW.

FELICIA: *(to INTERPRETER)* I thought YOU wanted to look at my passport. Always clarify who's talking, ok?

OFFICER SWALLOW: Is there something wrong?

INTERPRETER: No, sir.

OFFICER SWALLOW: Stop talking behind my back.

FELICIA: You're supposed to interpret what he said.

INTERPRETER: *(Discreet; in signs only)* He thought we were talking behind his back.

OFFICER SWALLOW: You are a citizen of Mexico, is that correct?

FELICIA: Yes.

OFFICER SWALLOW: State your last name, and then your first name.

INTERPRETER signs "state" literally.

FELICIA: California. Delgado, Felicia.

OFFICER SWALLOW: Delgado is your middle name?

FELICIA: Delgado is my last name.

OFFICER SWALLOW: What is California then?

FELICIA: California is my state.

OFFICER SWALLOW: I did not ask you for the name of your state.

FELICIA: You said state, last name, and first name.

OFFICER SWALLOW: I said "state your last name and then your first name."

FELICIA: The interpreter signed "state."

INTERPRETER: I-I-I apologize. I-I did sign "state" as in "there are fifty states in America." I should've signed "say your last name . . . ."

OFFICER SWALLOW: Yes, you should have. Is 8512 Camarillo Street, Los Angeles, California your current residence?

FELICIA: Are you asking the interpreter about his address?

OFFICER SWALLOW: No, I am asking you.

INTERPRETER: Are you asking me, sir?

FELICIA: Then, please look at me when asking questions.

OFFICER SWALLOW: *(looking at INTERPRETER)* I am looking at you.

INTERPRETER: Don't look at me—look at her.

OFFICER SWALLOW: But she can't hear me. What's the point?

FELICIA writes something on paper for SWALLOW. He reads as she writes.

OFFICER SWALLOW: "You should know interpreter like el robot—traducir informacion—help communicacion one-on-one." *(loudly)* Ok, El Robot! Is 8512 Camarillo Street, Los Angeles, California your current residence?

FELICIA: Yes.

OFFICER SWALLOW: Are you applying for a United States citizenship?

FELICIA: Yes.

OFFICER SWALLOW: Are you a citizen of Mexico?

FELICIA: Yes.

OFFICER SWALLOW: What is your current occupation?

FELICIA: Teacher of deaf.

INTERPRETER pronounces "deaf" as "death."

OFFICER SWALLOW: You teach about death. So, your occupation is mortuary science? Pathologist? Funeral service director? What?

INTERPRETER fingerspells and gestures each occupation.

FELICIA: I don't teach about death. I teach little deaf children.

INTERPRETER pronounces "deaf" as "death" again.

OFFICER SWALLOW: You teach little children about death? I repeat: What—is—your—occupation?

FELICIA writes something on paper and shows it to OFFICER SWALLOW. She glares at INTERPRETER.

OFFICER SWALLOW: I see. Teacher of deaf children. Ok. I am going to ask you some citizenship questions. What do—

The interpreter's cell phone rings.

INTERPRETER: Excuse me one moment . . . Hello? Yes. They have those in maroon? Oh goody! What?!? They gotta ship them all the way from Pakistan? How long will that take? Well, order two more while you're at it, hon. Yeah, gotta go. Love you. Bye.

An incredulous silence.

OFFICER SWALLOW: I repeat: What do the stars on the US flag represent?

FELICIA: Fifty states in America.

While OFFICER SWALLOW marks the application, she signs "thanks" sarcastically to INTERPRETER.

OFFICER SWALLOW: What is the first holiday celebrated by early Americans?

FELICIA: *(pause)* July 4th.

Naturalization

Wanting to help her out, INTERPRETER surreptitiously shakes his hand to warn her it is the wrong answer. Tell him, it's July 4th.

INTERPRETER: *(subtly; in signs only)* No, it's Thanksgiving.

FELICIA: What??

INTERPRETER: *(subtly; in signs only)* Turkey. Gobble-gobble.

OFFICER SWALLOW: I repeat: What is the first holiday celebrated by early Americans?

FELICIA: Thanksgiving.

OFFICER SWALLOW: I will now ask you to cite some lines from "The Star-Spangled Banner."

INTERPRETER translates the line as: "You look-at [i.e., sight] lines, flag." FELICIA stands, faces the flag with her back to OFFICER SWALLOW. Whenever you are ready. *(no response; louder)* I said, whenever you are ready.

INTERPRETER: Excuse me sir, she can't hear you.

OFFICER SWALLOW: *(loud)* I WILL NOW ASK YOU TO CITE SOME LINES FROM "THE STAR-SPANGLED BANNER."

INTERPRETER: Excuse me, sir, what I meant was she is death. She can't hear you at all.

OFFICER SWALLOW: Very well. *(Taps her on the shoulder.)* I will now ask you to cite some lines from "The Star-Spangled Banner."

FELICIA: I counted thirteen lines.

INTERPRETER: *(to FELICIA; signs only)* I think he means sing some lines from, you know, our national anthem?

FELICIA: Oh, I know some words . . . but I can't sing. Can you help me sing the words, please?

OFFICER SWALLOW: Is there a problem?

INTERPRETER: Translation snag. Just a minute, sir.

Naturalization

INTERPRETER: *(signs only)* Me? Sing??

FELICIA: *(to INTERPRETER)* If you sing and I sign, it might make him soft-hearted, and maybe give me my citizenship. Please, please, please??? *INTERPRETER nods his head.* Ready? Should I count 1, 2, 3?

INTERPRETER nods his head; clears his throat. OFFICER SWALLOW is puzzled by what is going on, but INTERPRETER reassures him with gestures of "Wait-for-it-it'll-be-good!" Words between brackets are lines that FELICIA forgets. INTERPRETER sings a magnificent and haunting, yet odd rendition of the song (since he has to scramble to cover what FELICIA forgot).

  Note: There are two ways to approach this. If the actor has a mellifluous voice, by all means go for beautiful and haunting. If the actor is not a good singer, then he should play the character attempting to belt out his best rendition of the song.

FELICIA will sign in the classic, sign-song/"beautiful-pictures-in-the-air" manner mixed with obvious gibberish during parts of the song that she does not know. It is a heart-melter from the hearing, nonsigners' point of view, but a knee-slapper from the signers' point of view.

FELICIA: 1, 2, 3, Oh, say can you see, by the dawn's early light, [What so proudly we hailed at the twilight's last gleaming?], [Whose broad stripes and bright stars through the perilous fight, O'er the ramparts] we watched, were so gallantly streaming? And the rockets' red glare, the bombs bursting in air, [Gave proof through the night that] our flag was still there. [O say, does that star-spangled banner yet wave. O'er the] land of the free and the home of the brave?

OFFICER SWALLOW: *He dabs his eyes with a handkerchief and clears his throat. We can't tell if he was moved by the "beauty" of her signs or wracked to tears (if applicable) by INTERPRETER's awful singing. Although there is more to the interview, he has seen and heard enough. He closes her case folder.* That was incredibly ... *(pause)* ... sorry, I have no words. Please step outside in the waiting area while a colleague double-checks the paperwork and prints out a copy of your application. We'll call you back shortly for the photographs.

FELICIA sits, closes her eyes, and crosses her fingers. INTERPRETER goes over to a nearby framed picture on the wall—perhaps the US president—combs his hair in the reflection, and grooms himself in anticipation of a photo op. His phone rings. Out of habit, he still signs and speaks.

INTERPRETER: Hello? Almost done. A terrible accident? Where? Emergency room? I've never interpreted at a hospital before. Ok, I'll try my best—be there pronto.

The End

2009

Burning Fat
—a monologue of a deaf actress

Setting: Gym; last bike in a row of bike machines; the present

Note: The role of Polly should be performed by a deaf actress fluent in American Sign Language. Polly's lines should be voiced by a hearing actress offstage, a prerecorded voice, or perhaps by another character spinning on a bike next to her.

Lights up on a deaf woman pedaling furiously on an exercise bike. She is in her forties, obviously "past her prime," in Hollywood's view. Out of breath, she takes a break and drinks from her water bottle.

POLLY: Some people say the meanest thing I've ever done was to use this deaf guy—a pale, skinny, doink-face with two earplugs and a body aid. Terrible signer—like a hearing person in ASL 1 class. Hey—I say, it was all business. He was a writer, sort of. Heard he wrote plays. Now you must understand that I'm a deaf actress. A pretty one, if I must say so myself. Now you know why I'm on the bike every day. Many people tell me that I look like Kathleen Quinlan. That actress in the film *I Never Promised You a Rose Garden*? If you can't remember that, then try *Apollo 13*. She played the astronaut's wife. Tom Hanks was the beleaguered hubby. She's brunette-like, angular face, dark angry eyes, and a dimple. But I've got double-dimples. Well, I was living in New York City when Doink arrived in DC. He moved there after graduating from some college in Chicago. He got a teaching position with the English department at Gallaudet University. We met once at a deaf convention where he was hired to write a short skit for entertainment night. It wasn't bad. I decided to look him up when I was in town. "Oh hi! I'm so glad we could get together. It's been a long time." He gives me that look like he's never seen me before—really, like he can't believe a woman is actually talking to him. Doink! "Hey, it's me, Polly! How is your playwriting coming along?" He blinked like a nerd and said he was doing fine. Got something produced way off-off-off-off-off Broadway. Like Mahwah, New Jersey maybe?? "Wonderful!" I said.

"Just wonderful." I'm gonna get this guy to write me some juicy roles like Mark Medoff did for Phyllis Fuckin' Frelich or Marlee Muthah Matlin. *Children of Lesser God.* I'm sure you know it. They've been on one long free ride. Right place, right time, I say. Lucky bitches! Excuse me . . . (*She adjusts the weight loss belt around her belly, which became undone.*) I gotta work on Doink nice and slow. A deaf writer like him oughta be able to write something decent for a deaf actress, right? Maybe he'll write something more authentic than Medoff. Medoff's hearing. He ain't got the deaf experience that Doink has. Nice and slow. Don't want him to know my motives. I suggested to him, "Why don't you send your plays to my partner. He's an artistic director for a small theatre company in New York. Maybe he can produce your work. Do you have anything for me and him to read?" Doink's eyes widen. I can see he's hungry for attention to his writing. He's been holed up in some room in front of the computer for so long. He wants the glory. I can see the hair on his arms stick up. His eyes all a-glitter. Oh girl—this guy is easy. But such a doink! Well, time to hop back on for another route. Let's see—Random . . . Hilly . . . Trail . . . aha, here it is—Fat Burn.

(*She tightens her weight loss belt and climbs onto the bike. She misses the saddle and falls forward, catching herself on the handlebars. Slowly, she begins to pedal, increasing in speed, but the ferocity is gone.*)

Lights to black.

May 2021

The Deaf Street Musician

Setting: A street corner with the proverbial hat or music case open for tips; the present.

Lights up on a homeless deaf person playing a small- or medium-sized musical instrument. Possible instruments: snare drum, bucket drum, thumb piano, jaw harp, or harmonica—or whatever the deaf actor may be musically talented with. The musician plays quite beautifully or impressively. A hearing person walks by, stops, and listens for a while, visibly impressed.

HEARING: Where did you learn to play? *(The musician keeps playing.)* Hey—where did you learn to play that? *(The musician notices someone talking; gestures "what?")* Where did you learn to play? *(The musician gestures not being able to hear.)* You're deaf!?

MUSICIAN: *(in voice and sign)* You're hearing!

HEARING: You speak!

MUSICIAN: You speak too!

HEARING: No way.

MUSICIAN: You're speaking now.

HEARING: I meant, no way you're deaf.

MUSICIAN: Well, I'm 75 percent deaf in my left ear and 90 percent deaf in my right ear. According to my audiogram, that makes me severely deaf.

HEARING: I'll be damned. And you can play a *(insert instrument name)*.

MUSICIAN: Well, what can you play?

HEARING: Play? You mean a musical instrument?

MUSICIAN: What else could I be referring to—my nuts? (*Gestures holding imaginary balls.*)

HEARING: Hahaha . . . you've got a sense of humor.

MUSICIAN: Do you have one?

HEARING: An organ or a sense of humor?

MUSICIAN: Either.

HEARING: You're really funny. (*laughs nervously*) Hahaha, say, are you reading my lips?

MUSICIAN: No.

HEARING: You're not? How do you understand what I'm saying?

MUSICIAN: What?

HEARING: How do you underst—

(*The musician nudges their tip container forward and returns to playing majestically.*)

Lights slowly go to black.

June 2020

The Hair Radar
—a short comedy

CIARA: Very animated and physical in the way she expresses herself. She is a big Black woman, cute and endearing, with a colorful personality that fills a room. She has a distinctive signing and voicing style.

SYDNEY: Thin, geeky, Black, bespectacled man; shorter than CIARA. Whenever CIARA makes a pun or sarcastic remark, she slaps or nudges him. He is her all-in-one punctuation mark, underscoring buddy, echo, slap pad, and straight man.

Note: It is imperative that the actors playing CIARA and SYDNEY be African American and Deaf. CIARA should be fluent in American Sign Language. Ideally, it would be great if the actor has the ability to Sim-Com (Simultaneous Communication, a challenging, sometimes politically incorrect skill of signing and speaking at the same time). If not, an offstage voice actor can speak her lines.

The actor for SYDNEY does not need to be fluent in ASL but his signing should be clear enough for the audience to understand his signs on stage. If the actor does not have that knack for Sim-Comming, then an offstage voice actor for him would work as well.

Since the characters have little or no experience with using a live microphone, comic potential could be explored with its use.

Time: Present.

Place: Karaoke stage with a microphone on a stand.

Lights up on CIARA and SYDNEY entering.

CIARA: Good evening, evrabody! My name's Ciara. Like "see" "air" "uh." And this is my good friend, Sydney. Sid—like "Sid the Science Kid" and "knee"—Sid-knee. Wait—you don't know Sid the Science Kid? Young cartoon character of color—got cool, funky purple hair, natural locks? On PBS Kids? Pah! Finally got a POC as lead character for cartoons. Anyhow, my sidekick here—name's Sydney, got it? (He ain't no Sydney Poitier!), right?

Slaps SYDNEY.

SYDNEY: Right! Ain't no Sydney Pointeeyeah. I'm just me.

CIARA: *(sings melodramatically to SYDNEY)* "To sirrrrr, with looooovvve!"

SYDNEY: You singing? . . . to me?

CIARA: No, no—just joshin'. *(to audience)* We're not gonna be singing no songs. We deaf—we can't sing for shit! But, we gonna sign and talk with you—equal rights, right?

Slaps him.

SYDNEY: Equal rights!

CIARA: You hearies get to come up here and sing your shit; we deafies get to sign our shit—fair?

SYDNEY: I think that's fair.

CIARA: Now it's our turn.

SYDNEY: Our turn!

CIARA: Somebody turn that TV off. We don't need your words, no music—we gonna make up our own, 'kay?

SYDNEY: That's right, our own words.

CIARA: Hey! Did j'all see Bob lately? He changed! I'm tellin' ya, he changed! Ain't dat right?

Slaps him.

SYDNEY: *(nods head)* You got dat right! Bob different.

CIARA: Ya know how I know? He cuts his hair every two weeks now. Two weeks!

SYDNEY: Two weeks!

The Hair Radar

CIARA: He never done that before. He always come to work *(gestures disheveled hair)*—bedhead! Don't care about how he look. Then he met A-mannnda!

SYDNEY: Yup—A-mannnda!

CIARA: I asked: "What up, Bob?" He say nuthin'. I go "nuthin"?? "Bullshit! Sumthin's up. You cut ya hair ever two weeks now. Summmmthin's up!"

SYDNEY: Sumpn's up.

CIARA: I go: "Bobby-baby, I been watchin' you—you cuttin' yo hair ever two weeks. 'Sup with dat??" He go: "Oh, nuthin', just gettin' a haircut, that's all." I go: "Ever two weeks??"

Slaps him.

SYDNEY: Yeah, two weeks?

CIARA: I know why! A-m-a-n-d-a.

SYDNEY: *(sing-songy, but terrible)* A-m-a-n-d-a!

CIARA: He don't say nuthin' but his face got real red when I said her name.

SYDNEY: Real red!

CIARA: I been watchin' Bob. I know he got the hots for Amanda. I think she do too.

SYDNEY: I seen it.

CIARA: She puttin' on a little more makeup now. A little this on her eyelashes. A little that on her lips, and whatnot. I go somewheres and there's Bob and Amanda close together in the same circle, wherever they go.

SYDNEY: Same circle.

CIARA: You think so?

SYDNEY: Yeah, they in same circle—it ain't no triangle.

The Hair Radar

CIARA: He never done that before. He always come to work *(gestures disheveled hair)*—bedhead! Don't care about how he look. Then he met A-mannnda!

SYDNEY: Yup—A-mannnda!

CIARA: I asked: "What up, Bob?" He say nuthin'. I go "nuthin"?? "Bullshit! Sumthin's up. You cut ya hair ever two weeks now. Summmmthin's up!"

SYDNEY: Sumpn's up.

CIARA: I go: "Bobby-baby, I been watchin' you—you cuttin' yo hair ever two weeks. 'Sup with dat??" He go: "Oh, nuthin', just gettin' a haircut, that's all." I go: "Ever two weeks??"

Slaps him.

SYDNEY: Yeah, two weeks?

CIARA: I know why! A-m-a-n-d-a.

SYDNEY: *(sing-songy, but terrible)* A-m-a-n-d-a!

CIARA: He don't say nuthin' but his face got real red when I said her name.

SYDNEY: Real red!

CIARA: I been watchin' Bob. I know he got the hots for Amanda. I think she do too.

SYDNEY: I seen it.

CIARA: She puttin' on a little more makeup now. A little this on her eyelashes. A little that on her lips, and whatnot. I go somewheres and there's Bob and Amanda close together in the same circle, wherever they go.

SYDNEY: Same circle.

CIARA: You think so?

SYDNEY: Yeah, they in same circle—it ain't no triangle.

99

CIARA: I thought so myself. You look at the staff meetings. Look where they sit at—rat next to each other—like dat: *(Gestures two pairs of legs together. SYDNEY tries to copy her but he's not fluent enough in ASL to get it right.)*

CIARA: You gotta put your fingers together. Parallel like this. You been signing for nine months—you should be gettin' this by now.

SYDNEY tries again.

CIARA: Close enuf—he gettin' there. You keep workin' at it. I still can't get over it. Bob and Amanda. Who woulda thunk it—them two together?

SYDNEY: Who woulda thunk it?

CIARA: I gonna keep ma eye on dem . . . see what happens down the road, ya know? Ding dong . . . . Hear sumthin'?

SYDNEY: What ya hearing?

CIARA: "I-do" bells.

SYDNEY: I do bells. What's that?

CIARA: *(Slaps him.)* C'mon boy—ya know. Dah dah da-da.

SYDNEY: Wedding bells?

CIARA: Bingo! Give that boy a prize teddy bear!

SYDNEY: I git it! I-do I-do . . . wedding vows.

CIARA: You know, I always stay focus on my work but I gots like a radar or something. I know when somebody's having a bad day. I see ma boss's hair sticking out like that. Watch out! She having a bad day. I don't even go in her office if her hair sticking out like that.

SYDNEY: Watch out!

CIARA: You don't wanna cross her path. She cut you to pieces—snip snip snip. Pieces of youse all over da place.

SYDNEY: Snip snip snip—scattered all over.

CIARA: I see another staff member. I look through her office window. If I see her writing like this *(gestures writing really fast and hard)* I back off. I back way da fuck off.

SYDNEY: Back way da fuck off!

CIARA: See her scribble hard like dat with her pen, she having a bad day. I know. I been watching her a whole year. Know evrabody's bad days. I got it down pat up here.

SYDNEY: She got it all up there.

CIARA: Know how I know fer sure?

SYDNEY: How?

CIARA: Look at the hair. There'll be sumthin' off. That girl that was scribblin' hard? Her hair looked dull and clumpy—like she was in a hurry to get to work, so she spit on her comb to straighten her hair.

SYDNEY: Ah, a comb spitter!

CIARA: If I see you have a bad day, I leave you alone. If I'm supposed to ask you a question or give you something, I just write a note and leave it on the door or leave something in your box. I ain't gonna mess with your bad day. I unnerstand that. Evrabody got bad days. I gets 'em too. When I gets one, I go nuclear—don't go near me. I radioactive, you feel me?

SYDNEY: Oh yeah, she get real radioactive!

CIARA: When I got a bad day, you better get youself to a bomb shelter! Cuz I explode something really, really big. BOOOM! The walls come tumbling down.

SYDNEY: BOOM!

CIARA: Humpty Dumpty gonna fall down big time! You hear what I'm sayin'?

SYDNEY: I hear ya—I mean I see ya.

CIARA: Moral of story—stay in your bomb shelter till I'm over my bad day.

SYDNEY: How we know when you over your bad day?

CIARA: Look at my hair, boy! What else? You see it nice and fixed up, you know I'm having a good day. You see me all nappy and shit— hair ever which way? Zoom to da bomb shelter! Got it?

SYDNEY: I got it, I got it—zoom to da bombshelter.

CIARA: You see my hair all pretty, It's the all-clear bell, unnerstand? All clear, evrabody—c'mon out. Ciara's bad day is gonnnne!

SYDNEY: Ciara's bad day gonnnnnne!

CIARA: No, ya gotta sing it, brother!

SYDNEY: *(tries but doesn't quite have it)* Ciara's bad day goonnnnne!

CIARA: Ya gotta do the all clear before that.

SYDNEY tries to imitate the all-clear sound but it comes out wimpy.

CIARA: We'll work on that some other time. Now let's see what kinda day people in the audience are having. *(She points out certain people in the audience. Improvises and reacts to people's hair styles.)* She's having a good day . . . he's having a good day . . . she a good day, he a good day, oh I like your hair—very nice the way you got that done . . . good day there, good day over there—wow, love that style, very nice! Ohhh . . . that is super nice! That's not only a good day, that's a weeklong vacay!

SYDNEY: Weeklong vacay!

CIARA: Oh, another nice one over here—definitely a good day . . . uh oh! . . . back off . . . Bad Day Alert! *(Picks out someone whose hair doesn't look all that good to her. She gestures whatever does not look right—a bad comb-over, a bedhead, a bald head, a colored wig or brightly dyed hair, a nasty weave, or whatever the actor can play off of.)*

SYDNEY: Bad Day Alert!

The Hair Radar

CIARA: I'm so sorry you're having a bad day. Evrabody, back away. Give some space. I tell ya what I'm a gonna do—I gonna buy you a drink. A attitude adjustment *(she plays with the alliterative signs for "attitude" and "adjustment")* is what you need.

SYDNEY: Yeah, attitude adjustment.

CIARA: Matter o' fact—why not evrabody help? Buy this person a drink. Turn that bad day to a vacay.

SYDNEY: Bad day to vacay!

CIARA: Well, I think our time's up—about the same amount you hearies take to sing a song, right? Y'all have a good day, hear? Take good care 'a your hair!

SYDNEY: Take care a yur hair, y'all!

The End

June 2021

Toxic Flower
—a monodrama

The present. Garden department of a big box store. A projection screen is set up with a laptop and projector in an aisle flanked by assorted plants and flowers. If a laptop-projector setup is not available, plant props could be used (and passed around) for demonstration.

DAFF, the supervisor, is busy setting things up for her first meeting with newly hired deaf employees. While she is prepping, she eats sunflower seeds from a bag.

There is a slide up on the screen [or a banner] that reads:

"Welcome to Humble Abode Hardware Deaf Employees Orientation: Garden Department."

DAFF: *(reviewing her list)* One, two, three, four, five . . . Hamilton? I'll call you, Ham, for short, alright? You're big and beefy—it fits. And you're Amelia, yes? Great! I'll put you down as Amy. Easier to finger-spell. And you must be Elizabeth. Will call you Liz—perfect! Hmmm, I don't see your name on the list. Just hired this morning? Oh, ok. See me after the meeting. Two others are not here yet. Too bad! I must start now because the other departments have their orientations after this one and you're not supposed to miss them. But I'll tell you one thing, mine'll be the best. Mmmmm, these sunflower seeds are good. Anyone want some? No? They have lots of vitamins—good for your immune system.

Ok, my name is Daffy, or Daff for short. Real name is Daffodil; sign name flower-in-hair. Why? You guessed it—I love wearing a flower in my hair.

So, this is MY department. I'm the only deaf supervisor here at Humble Abode Hardware—HAH, for short. Welcome to HAH! As you probably saw from the Tools department orientation, there are 158 HAHs across the country. They are very good at recruiting deaf employees. Why? The owner's mother was deaf, so he always makes a point that every new store that opens must reach out to the Deaf community to offer employment.

My background? I have a bachelor of science degree in botany. In case you may not know, that's the study of plants. Guess I'm in the right place, huh? I was supposed to go to grad school to get my PhD but that didn't work out. Long story. I won't bore you with it. I'm happy working here in my little world of gardening.

I know that all of you won't be working in my department all the time. HAH likes to rotate their employees so that they don't get bored in one department. Stupid, but not my philosophy. Whatever the boss wants. So here in Flowers and Plants I've got the outdoor plants in full sunshine, the semi-indoor ones in partial shade, and the inside ones needing full shade. I have various kinds of soil, fertilizers, and chemicals in aisles 1 and 2. Pots, garden tools, wheelbarrows in aisles 3 and 4. Hoses, attachments, watering cans, and all that kind of stuff in aisle 5.

Now pay close attention, this is very import—is Ham asleep?

She grabs a squirt bottle and spritzes a stream of water at Ham.

Fall asleep again—I'll have you fired immediately. Now, I'm going to show all of you pictures and the names of five flowers we carry that are poisonous. Yes, very dangerous. They look deceptively beautiful, but you must be very careful around them. I know it's silly to think—you're not going to be eating them, but you can imagine a young mother with a child pushing a stroller or a kid walking by. The child grabs the petal of a beautiful flower and puts it in her mouth. Finish! Dead kid. Call the funeral home. Alright, here we go:

Advances slides on screen.

This is Daphne. It's a semievergreen shrub with clusters of small and fragrant rose, white, or purple flowers. Grows mostly in the southern United States. Daphnin and mezerine are the poisons in this plant. The strongest poison is in the berries and sap. Eating this plant can cause convulsions, headaches, and in severe cases coma and death. (Public service announcement . . . If you really hate your kid, it only takes two berries to kill him . . . wink-wink.)

Toxic Flower

She grabs a handful of sunflower seeds and throws them at Liz and Amy.

Liz, Amy—you two have a question? If you've got something to say, come up here and ask. Nothing? Then, stop your yakking while I'm sharing important information that impacts our company and customers.

Here is Nightshade (ak.a. belladonna). The toxins in this plant have been known since the time of the Roman Empire when they were used by ancient Romans to poison enemies. The flowers of this plant are small, reddish purple and tubular shaped. The berries are the deadliest part of the plant. The atropine found in belladonna disrupts the nervous system and can destroy the body's ability to control breathing and heart rate, leading to death. (If you hate your spouse, now there's a plant for you!)

That is angel's trumpet. Don't be fooled by the name of this plant—it's certainly no angel. Angel's trumpet is a shrub or small tree showing trumpet-shaped petals in many colors. It contains scopolamine and atropine, two hallucinogens and poisons. The entire plant is poisonous with the highest concentration of toxins in the seeds. Side effects? Hallucinations, coma, and delirium. Some Amazonian tribes use this plant as a hallucinogen in rituals, but an overdose can be fatal. (If you want to get high, . . . please at home, not on the job!)

These are azaleas—a very popular ornamental shrubs. Your parents or grandparents probably have them in their front yards. I have some myself. You can see that they have large, attractive clusters of flowers in pink, orange, red, white, and lavender. This plant contains andromedotoxins, which cause pain, nausea, paralysis, and sometimes death. All parts of the plant are deadly. Even honey from this plant can be toxic—the Greeks called it "mad honey" after observing Greek soldiers that had eaten it and gone crazy. When I was little, hearing kids in neighborhood would call me Deaf Daffy. I hated that! Wish I knew about azaleas back then . . . smirk . . . smirk.

This is hemlock. Its flowers are tiny and white, appearing in clusters atop tall carrot-like foliage. It looks like Queen Anne's lace. It is often confused with wild carrot. When eaten, it causes death. It has coniine and pyridine—poisons that can bring on convulsions, coma, and death from respiratory failure. Greek criminals were killed off by being forced to drink hemlock juice. You know, Socrates, the famous Greek philosopher? He ended his life by drinking the juice. If you've had enough of your own life and want to end it—hemlock is your friend!

Now, when you start working in my department, I expect you to be prompt and follow my directions. Don't play games with me. Just because you're deaf and I'm deaf doesn't mean I'm easy to take advantage of. If I catch you playing any games with me, watch out. You don't know what I'm capable of.

She holds up pruning shears and squeezes the blades back and forth for emphasis.

The daffodil in her hair falls out. She fastens it back to her hair.

By the way, did I tell you that daffodils are poisonous? People sometimes mistake them for chives when cooking. Can cause serious stomach problems and possibly death. Don't get any funny ideas if you ever invite me over for dinner. Hahaha!

Well, anyhow, that concludes my presentation. If you have any questions, feel free to see me anytime. I'm always around.

Blackout.

June 2022

STORIES

Every Man Must Fall

The E.R.

When called to the emergency room, you will most likely get one of the follow-
ing cases to photograph: rape, child abuse, domestic violence, and police brutal-
ity. You MUST shoot the injured areas and the face in the same photo. When
shooting, vary the flash angle to reveal the bumps, bruises, and cuts. Be sure
to shoot lots of pictures—it would be disastrous to undershoot when it comes to
medical-legal situations. Each slide must be hand-labeled with your signature
and date on the back in case you get called to court to testify that you were
the photographer on the case. Hand deliver the photos to the requesting physi-
cian and have him sign your log to show proof that the images were delivered.
NEVER give the photos to a lawyer, a patient, or a police officer; they must
ask the physician for copies.

—from the *Student Preparation Manual for Examination as Registered*
Biological Photographers

When Max was told what the announcement over Dulaney High's
public address system was all about—that his friend, Billy Hendricks,
had drowned in the Loch Raven Reservoir—all he could do was sit
there and stare at the wooden speaker above the door. How could such
tragic news spill through the speaker's fabric screen and yet nothing
could be seen coming out. Max was of a world where all information
had to come to him visually. Most of his classmates and teachers never
understood that, despite repeated attempts to explain the realities of
his deafness.

Minutes before Max learned of the tragedy, the sun was shining
bright and cheerful rays into the classroom. Morning announcements
went on dreadfully long, and to him they sounded like an alley dog
barking incessantly. Since he couldn't lipread dogs and knew dogs
couldn't enunciate anything better than an "arf," "yap," or "rowf,"
Max ignored the morning cacophony and killed time playing tic-tac-
toe tournaments with Flathead, his desk-neighbor.

Flathead used condoms with see-through packages for "o's" while
Max put down twisted paper clips for "x's." The tourney winner
would get a six-pack of beer. Flathead was about to drop an "o" to

win a game when he suddenly stopped midway, pressing the condom between his fingers. He looked up at the doorway. Max could tell he was listening to the speaker by the way he tilted his head. Max imagined that if Flathead turned at the proper angle, a stream of words would enter cleanly into his ear, like water through a funnel. Max envied him for getting information that easily.

Flathead put the condom down and bowed his head. Max saw students behind him talking rapidly to each other. Others sat quietly, wide-eyed and slack-jawed. A few of the girls began to weep. One girl got up and walked hurriedly out of the classroom. Max looked over to Mr. Crumwell, his homeroom teacher, for some visual reference. Crumwell looked up toward the speaker, shook his head in disgust, mumbled something that looked like "he asked for it," and went back to grading papers. Somebody in the senior class must've gotten caught in the lavatory for smoking pot and wasn't going to be able to graduate—probably the star varsity pitcher or quarterback.

Max nudged Flathead's skinny arm. Flathead looked up at Max, all sad-eyed, running his hand over his crew top, soothing himself. Max gave him a questioning gesture with an upward shake of his head, asking, "What's up?"

Max knew something more serious than a pot bust had happened. Flathead didn't get emotional unless he won at tic-tac-toe or lined up a hot date for a mixer. He flipped the tic-tac-toe sheet over, grabbed the pencil and wrote, "Billy Hendricks died."

Max had to read it a few times. Flathead couldn't spell to save his life, and Max wondered if he wrote an incomplete sentence like, "Billy Hendricks did."

To confirm the spelling, Max whispered, "Are you saying Billy Hendricks d-i-e-d?"

Mr. Crumwell and the students in the front of the class suddenly turned their heads to look at Max. He thought he had whispered.

Flathead's lips quivered. He scrawled the words, "drowned, lock ravin."

It was then that Max took a good hard look at the loudspeaker with the coarse fabric covering its front, wishing that somehow captions could come out of it during announcements. Perhaps no one would think this was such a big deal, but Max wanted the right to get the news at the same time as everyone else, especially news concerning someone he cared about.

This was the first experience with death that had affected Max. When one of the boys in his Cub Scout troop, a kid with asthma, had died, it had not shaken him. The kid was a snob. Only a year ahead of him in elementary school, the boy always acted like he was more intelligent and talented. Max felt as if the kid perceived him as slow and suspected it was because of his deafness. Max didn't know why the kid thought he was such hot shit, because whenever the troop played baseball, the kid had to take a puff from his inhaler between empty swings at the plate. And here was Max, knocking balls over the stone wall in left field, rounding the bases as easy as breathing in his sleep.

One October evening at home, Max was helping his mother carve a pumpkin in preparation for a Scout meeting. She was the troop's den mother. His mother received a phone call that brought tears to her eyes. He was told later that the call was about the asthmatic troop member. The kid simply couldn't get enough oxygen and had died the previous day. How could anyone not have enough air? There's so much of it outside. Max asked his mother about this later, but she shrugged him off and dabbed her eyes again with a Kleenex. Now this one he really couldn't figure out. The kid wasn't her son.

Max approached Mr. Crumwell and asked to be excused. He was feeling all knotty inside and needed some air and water. Thankfully, there wasn't anybody in the lavatory. He didn't know what he was going to feel, but whatever it was, he wanted to feel it alone without anyone scrutinizing his facial expressions or listening to sounds he might make. He clogged the drain with some paper towels and turned on the cold water to fill the sink up to the top. He lowered his face into the water until numbness from the cold came over him. He tried to envision what Billy's face must've looked like under water. Bloated? White? Smiling? Yawning, maybe?

Max couldn't believe his buddy was killed by a substance so weak and insubstantial as water—dead from the very thing they worked with. Billy and Max worked side by side as dishwashers on Saturdays and Sundays at the White Coffee Pot, a family restaurant nestled between Read's Drugstore and Hardware Fair in a strip mall. Billy was the kind of guy who would probably grow up to be a Klan member or the president of the local chapter of the NRA. His blazing orange hair matched a hunter's outdoor shirt, and a badly chipped front tooth gave him a smile that showed you something was missing. Although he was only seventeen years old, he had the belly of a beer drinker.

After six months of working together at the White Coffee Pot, Billy got fired. Max found out why when Sylvia, the manager, called him out of the kitchen and had him sit across from her in one of the black Naugahyde booths. She stared at him a long time before saying a word. Max mentally ran through a list of all the things that he shouldn't have done in the back: dipping his fingers in the cornbread batter, taking crab cakes home, squirting the dishwasher hose at a waitress's legs, or neglecting to mop the floor on the late nights when he was tired and alone.

Overenunciating a bit for his benefit, Sylvia asked, "Have you ever looked down into the women's restroom?" When she said "down" her jaw dropped low enough for him to see that she had spent a lot of time in a dental office getting her teeth filled with gold.

"Looked down? I'm sorry, I don't know what you're talking about."

"You've never, ever looked down in the women's restroom??"

"The only time I even look in there is when I empty the trash can and mop the floor after we close. What happened?"

"You honestly don't know?" She put her index finger to her head to emphasize the word "know" in hopes that it might rouse his memory. The gesture made Max feel like he was deaf-and-dumb.

"No ma'am," he said, using his best speech. "I swear." During this line of questioning, he leaned forward on the table and stroked his chin. He had read in a book about body language that this posture would show that he was seriously thinking about what the other person was saying. Max hid his other hand under the table, keeping it busy exploring hardened pieces of bubble gum, nuts and bolts, a carved-out hole. . . . Then, finally he grasped what she was asking.

Once Billy had invited him up in the rafters to take a peek in the ladies' room. He said he cut out a small hole in the corner of the ceiling—small enough that no one inside could really notice it but large enough so that someone outside could see everything that went on inside. Virtuously, he told Billy he wasn't interested. Max tried to sound cool and not so hard up to see female anatomy. Actually, he made a note to himself to check it out one day when he was the sole dishwasher on a weekend. The very next time he worked alone, an opportunity presented itself. The restaurant was closed and it was just him, Esther the cook, and a couple of waitresses cleaning up. Esther was about forty, with a pockmarked face and a body pushing against an extra-large cook's uniform. She put down her grill scrub brush and apron, and headed for the back.

Max quickly went over to the walk-in refrigerator pretending to stock up on "prep" foods for the next day. He timed opening the refrigerator just as Esther opened the door to the ladies' room. He closed the walk-in quietly without going inside and went up the ladder.

There were greasy handprints on the ceiling tiles where Billy had pushed them aside to gain access. Max's heart was beating fast since he wouldn't be able to hear if one of the waitresses came by. He put his hand up to the same corner where Billy's handprints were found, noticing that Billy's hands were smaller than his. Amazing how an ego exaggerated one's size.

Cartons of lettuce, tomatoes, and potatoes were down below the ladder waiting to be stored in the walk-in. Max looked once more at the ceiling tile, paused, and then came back down the ladder. He had enough of a stigma being deaf. If caught, he would never get another job in his entire life. He visualized the rumors that would spread about the incompetencies and sexual vagaries of deaf people.

Across from him in the booth, Sylvia lit up a filterless Pall Mall. She politely bent her head down to spit out some loose tobacco strands in the direction of her lap. Each "spphht" was followed by a puff of smoke.

"Well, I just fired Mr. Hendricks for lewd behavior in the back." She drew a heavy sigh and exhaled another column of smoke.

"Oh, really?" He stifled the urge to grab a napkin from the dispenser to tear apart and roll up into little balls to calm his nerves.

"I went in the back the other day to check out how many crab cakes we had left in the walk-in."

"Y-yeah," he answered, not sure if she was asking him a question.

"Well, I saw where that ladder was when I came out of the walk-in. Mr. Hendricks was standing on it, half up in the ceiling looking down into the women's restroom."

"Oh my God," said Max, slapping his forehead to demonstrate disapproval.

Sylvia ended her interrogation the same way she had opened it, with an eagle-eyed stare. He was innocent, of course, but he was afraid that his knowledge of the hole would trip this human lie detector. Finally, Sylvia put out her cigarette in the white ashtray shaped like a coffee pot and slid out of the booth. Max grabbed a napkin and quickly rolled a couple of little paper balls between his fingertips before going back to the dishes.

At school, Billy and Max happened to be in the same photography class. Billy said he took photography to get out of his art requirement. He couldn't stand the idea of sitting on a stool for two hours slapping paint onto a canvas; that was for girls, and boys who wanted to be girls.

Since there weren't enough darkrooms to go around, they shared one. Billy picked Max for a partner because of Max's premature baldness. In Billy's mind, that meant Max was the most mature student around who wouldn't give a flick about what was said or done. Besides, Max was deaf and pretty much kept to himself. All Billy wanted to do was read *Playboy* magazines under the seedy illumination of a safelight.

Max ended up doing Billy's black-and-white prints. In exchange, Billy worked at the restaurant in Max's place any time he needed a Saturday or Sunday off to spend with his girlfriend who lived an hour and a half away.

Filling in at the restaurant wasn't the only reason why Max was willing to develop Billy's prints. The fat sucker had a damn good eye for composition and God only knew where he got it from. Billy's mother ran the laundromat at the end of the shopping center. All she did was open the place, made sure nobody walked out with a washer or dryer, locked up at closing time, and hurried home to watch "Dialing for Dollars" by the telephone. His father worked for the highway department filling potholes and striping yellow lines on the streets of Baltimore. He also ran the plow and salt truck during the winter when it snowed. His parents definitely didn't seem to carry any genes for a good eye in photographic composition.

In the most ordinary subjects, Billy found something extraordinary—like he'd shoot a rusty nail on a barn door. Big funky deal, right? In the developer bath, that 8 × 10-inch print came out looking like a Walker Evans or Dorothea Lange masterpiece from the Depression era. Max's pictures always ended up looking like cliches; the proverbial sunset smack dab in the middle of a print with the requisite seagull silhouetted against the sky.

Billy used his grandfather's old Leica range finder, the kind where you looked through the viewfinder from the upper left corner of the camera. Max didn't know how Billy did it since range finders never recorded exactly what was seen through the glass. Max's pictures were always off-center whenever he shot with that kind of camera.

When Billy went shooting, he "burned" film. He'd shoot up a roll of thirty-six exposures on that one rusty nail whereas Max hated to waste more than two frames on a subject.

"Billy, where did you learn to shoot like that?" Max would ask.

"Nowheres. I just aim and click, is all."

"But, there's more to it than that. I mean, how did you come up with stuff like taking pictures of water reflections and then turning the photos upside down to make your images look like the real thing?"

"Shit-if-I-know, man," Billy would say, holding his *Playboy* centerfold up vertically for a minute.

"I've never seen anybody turn their reflections upside-down. That's ingenious! You're a regular Monet, painting with your camera."

"What're you talking about money for?" he asked.

"Mo—nay."

"What is it? Some kind of an eel or sumthin'?" Then, he would give Max that chipped-tooth smile.

Max suspected Billy knew he was an artist but would never let on to anyone. Art was for sissies and for some reason Billy had a backwoods, tobacco-chewing reputation to maintain.

After the day Billy was fired, Max didn't see him much. He stopped going to photography classes. His blue, souped-up '62 Valiant with the small Confederate flag on the aerial was rarely seen about town. Max missed Billy's brazen presence but was so caught up in the end-of-the-year school activities that he almost forgot about Billy—until the morning of the death announcement.

Several months after Billy died, Max went fishing for old time's sake at the Loch Raven Reservoir under a Fourth of July sky that was as blue as it could ever get. He stood in the water up to his knees, holding the line of his bamboo rod out by the deep pocket where he knew sunfish liked to hang out. Max kept an eye on the red-and-white bobber, waiting for it to be pulled under. He and Billy used to troll in the area of Goetze's Cove for sunfish on Fourth of July weekends when they got time off from work. Whenever a catfish snatched onto Billy's line, he ripped the hook out of its mouth, replaced it with a lit firecracker, and heaved it in the air to explode like a grenade.

"What did you do that for, Bill?"

"Doin' my part for wildlife conservation."

"Man, you're a piece of wildlife. What's your part?"

"Keepin' the ugly fish population down. It's a bottom-feeder. You ever ate one of them?"

"No."

"Tastes like a dirty dishrag from all that shit it sucks up from the lake bottom."

"Yeah, right, Bill, I guess you would know the flavor of dirty dishrags."

Up on the bank of the cove was the granite, big as an old one-door refrigerator laying on its side. Max always thought of it as Billy's rock. According to the local news, this was near where Billy's body was pulled out of the water. It was at the rock that Max first saw Billy, after moving to the area. A small crowd of kids by the granite were yelling at Billy not to do whatever it was he was doing. He was a skinny little runt then. As Max snuck in for a closer view, he saw Billy pounding something against the rock over and over—a box turtle with its shell cracked apart and blood dripping out. Besides this prepubescent act of violence, what also stunned Max was the cloud-colored, gelatinous remains of the tortoise. He never realized turtles had a lump of jelly under their shells. And there was Billy grinning at this wondrous discovery, his eyes sparkling in the late afternoon sun. Max couldn't remember if his friend had the chip in his tooth then. In later years, Billy claimed he held his secret M.P.A. club meetings at the rock.

"What's M.P.A. stand for, Bill?"

"I ain't gonna tell you. You ain't a member."

Max wondered if Billy's club had any members at all. One of the neighborhood kids told Max in confidence that M.P.A. stood for Mashed Potatoes Association. It wasn't until the time when Billy and Max worked together at the White Coffee Pot that the potato connection was made. Billy craved mashed potatoes with a crater of butter and always kept a plate of them on the side while washing dishes.

The bobber continued to float in place, the white half still above the water. About three feet away, an object underwater reflected the sunlight. Max tried to edge toward it but kept slipping on smooth algae-covered rocks. He didn't want some crayfish snapping at his toes. If Billy was looking down on him at that moment and knew his thoughts, he would think that was awful sissified of him. In his head, he gave Billy the finger.

Max lowered the bamboo pole and tried to probe the object. Attached to it was a dark strap wavering in the water. Max caught the strap with the pole and retracted it. The strap slid off. He dipped the pole under and fished for the strap again. The object felt heavy and metallic as Max finally pulled it up.

It was a Leica range finder. Max swung the pole over and eased the camera on the bank. After cleaning the mud off, he could see that the film's counter was on "13." The rewind knob was taut indicating that there was indeed film inside. He took the camera home and kept it submerged in a sink of water to preserve the film until it could be brought to school the next morning for processing.

Not many people were at the photo lab since it was summer school. In the darkroom, Max got the absurd feeling that if he opened the camera back, minnows would flop out, but all that did was musty water. He developed the film and after fifteen minutes turned the lights on. The moldy smell was replaced by the vinegary odor of photographic chemicals. He washed the film and held it up to the bare bulb overhead. Twelve frames had been exposed of somebody's face, all looking similar, perhaps a man's face—hard to tell since these were negative images. The film was dried, cut into strips, and put into protective sleeves. Max took out a strip and inserted it into the enlarger.

He cranked the enlarger to blow the image up to an 8 × 10 size. He made an exposure and slipped the print into the developer. As he rocked the tray back and forth to agitate the chemicals, the image of Billy appeared on the paper. He wasn't smiling, yawning, or giving that devil-may-care look of his. The look was more like a downed US fighter pilot held as a POW during the Vietnam War. Billy's right eye was black and swollen shut. Across his forehead was a caterpillar-shaped gash. His nose had the unmistakable curve of a break in the middle. A thin but deep-looking cut on his chin showed that he was probably knifed. Both cheeks were swollen. His good eye looked dead-dull.

Max's heart rate became rapid and his throat went dry. He leaned over the darkroom sink and drank water from the faucet. He took the print out of the developer and bathed it in the other chemicals before continuing to wash the image of Billy Hendricks. Even though he was dead, Max felt comforted by the thought that he was cleansing Billy's wounds. Maybe no one was able to do this for him at the time. But what happened? Did Billy take these himself on a self-timer or did some bruiser shoot the pictures to record his handiwork and forgot to take the film out? Max couldn't tell from the background where the photos were taken. It was all white, probably a wall by the way the shadows fell behind Billy.

More prints were made from the rest of the negatives. All turned out basically the same except that the angles were slightly different in each frame. One shot was a little tilted. Another a little higher. A third, a bit to the left, and so forth. But, in all of them, Billy had that straight-ahead dead stare at the lens. It was a look Max had never seen in any of Billy's most mischievous moments.

Max cleaned and dried up everything in the darkroom. He decided not to show the prints to anyone in the lab and walked home contemplating what to do with this newfound evidence. He didn't want to take the pictures to Billy's parents, suspicious that Billy's father might be involved in this somehow. Billy and his father never got on and often wound up having fistfights in their backyard. Billy once said that when his old man got older, he was going to do to him what he had done to the turtle—crack the old man's skull and expose the jelly underneath that tough exterior.

If Max went to the cops, they'd go into some full-blown investigation, probing into everybody's lives and turning everything upside-down. Max resisted the need to show the pictures to people because he was well aware of their fickle nature of blabbing away secrets.

Fortunately, Max's parents weren't home yet. He pushed his mother's plants aside on the windowsill and opened the kitchen window. He moved the dirty dishes and glasses out of the sink and set them on the counter. He lifted the negatives and prints out of the box and set them by the sink. The soft light coming through the window made Billy look more vulnerable. It made him think of that song, *I Shall Be Released*, they always sang at Young Life meetings during junior high school. Max never really associated its meaning with anything until now, although he assumed they were singing about Jesus Christ after he read the lyrics his mother wrote down for him. "They say every man needs protection . . . they say that every man must fall." He felt all knotty again in his eyes and throat.

Max got a box of wooden matches out of the drawer and struck one. Suspending the prints and negatives over the sink, he held the match up to the corner of the photos, watching the flame grow big. The papers curled and the plastic sizzled. On the 8 × 10, the black around Billy's swollen eye grew bigger until it was black all over. Just when Max could no longer stand the heat, he dropped the images in the sink and waited until they were reduced to ashes. He brushed the soot down the drain and put in the drain plug. Turning on the hot water and squeezing in some detergent, he transferred the dirty tableware back into the sink. Then grabbing a sponge, Max began to wash the dishes.

2002

A Photographic Memory

Slip on the surgical hood. Tie the strings of the face mask together over the hood. Tuck in the scrub shirt. Pull the drawstrings of the pants tighter. Slip on the disposable shoe covers. Check the reflection in the full-length mirror to be sure everything looks right . . . *a green alien with white fluorescent lights protruding from the head* . . . check the camera. Make sure the film's sprocket holes are caught on the pins of the take-up spool. Click. Whirr. Click. Whirr. The film advances twice, the counter showing "1" through the tiny window. Motor drive's working fine. Turn on the flash unit. Hope these batteries are juiced up. Pull out some extras from the bag and put them in the back pocket, just in case. Press the test button. Pop. Press again. Pop . . . *sucker's loaded all right. Everything goes blind-white and loses its color. I blink at ghostlike negative images, floating in circles before me. Lockers. Overhead fluorescent lights. Wooden benches. Soiled towels. A positive image zooms up the middle—a naked, dry, beating heart. No protective sac surrounding it. And no luster. Suddenly, it ceases pumping and begins to harden, peel, and crack. Quickly, it breaks apart like an egg and spews an ooze of oil-black veins . . . .* I shut my eyes and curse myself for forgetting to look away when test-firing my flash unit.

Rings of perspiration begin to form at my armpits. My stomach churns and my scrotum shrivels, one controlling the other . . . *why couldn't this call have come while I'm out on lunch break? Why now when none of the other photographers are on hand? Why not on my day off? Why? Why? Why?* . . . Hey! Relax, boy. Take a deep breath. Sigh. All set . . . *or so you think.*

Out of the locker room and into a vestibule with double doors. A faded sign on the door says, "SURGICAL ATTIRE MUST BE WORN BEYOND THIS POINT!" An electric eye's vision is blocked and instantly the doors swing open for me . . . *whoa! Am I walking in an A&P store?? Those doors could've fooled me* . . . Hold the camera close so it doesn't sway and bang. I enter the long, glistening white-tiled corridor of operating suites, thinking how weird it is to be drugged and having your body rolled through this place on its back. Especially in this aseptic atmosphere reeking of antibacterial disinfectant.

Several green aliens are turning the corner, one pushing a small dinosaur—*a what? Oh!* A portable x-ray machine. Another pushes open the door to the patient holding room lined with beds and life support machines attached to wax figures . . . *God, how I wish there was some time to have my pre-op discussion with the surgeons in #3. They're not gonna know about the set of hand signals and gestures I've developed. I've gotta convince them I take pictures just as well as anyone in my profession, sometimes better!* . . . "Whoops! Excuse me." A different alien approaches fast, signaling for me to move out of the way. She pushes a motionless figure to an operating room to have its life restored, or make an attempt to.

I arrive at the first set of operating rooms and notice surgical tape labels slapped on each door. The operating procedures are handwritten on the tape strips.

OR #1: APPENDECTOMY—A nurse opens the door and drops a bundle of green sheets, splotched with rust color, on the floor to be picked up and laundered for the umpteenth time.

OR #2: DOUBLE-BARREL COLOSTOMY—Well, let's take a peek through the window to see if, by chance, they're rebuilding the double-barrel carburetor of a Chevy, hahahaha. The camera slips out of my hands and bangs against the door. Immediately the OR crew stops, lays down their tools, and looks toward the door. Duck! And keep walking! Geez, this feels like a Groucho Marx walk.

OR #3: CORONARY BYPASS—Breathe deep. My stomach gurgles . . . *either I walk in and suffer the consequences, or my department gets a bad reputation for not sending in a photographer* . . . Exhale. Inhale. Fiber from my face mask sticks to my tongue.

Enter. A look at the wall—a Simplex clock. Time is not so simple here—10:29 a.m. Huddled like football players on a sterile field, a team of three cardiac surgeons, an anesthesiologist, a scrub nurse, and a circulating nurse surround the coronary-stricken patient. Another person on the sidelines sits on a stool adjusting a complicated contraption of dials, switches, wires, and plastic tubing—the heart/lung machine.

A few heads turn and acknowledge my presence . . . *with masks on, they are . . . yes, that's it—praying mantises with swollen mandibles chewing on their prey. Or is it preying mantises? Their eyebrows are caterpillars backing away from each other, jumping an inch or two when there is a change of surgical procedure or when the mantises quickly turn to another helpless victim . . .* I'll never know if the doctors are telling me to get ready, or discussing the faulty coronary artery, or shooting the breeze about last weekend. Snap out of it! Warm up the flash unit. Attach the sync cords to the camera body. My hands are all sweaty. The muscles in my fingers twitch involuntarily. Simplex says 10:45. Deep breaths now.

The circulating nurse leaves the huddle. She looks over at me and at the same time appears to be chewing on something . . . *is she chewing gum? A greeting of "How are ya?" Or is she asking, "What's that you have there?" I smile and nod in hopes the gesture will satisfy her questions, if they were questions. Did she see me smile? You turkey! C'mon, you have a mask on. I want to say something but am afraid of getting into a conversation I can neither continue nor understand. Maybe I should just wave, huh? Nah, that's absurd . . .* The nurse shrugs her shoulders in exasperation, turns around, and fills the gap that she left in the huddle. I wonder if I'm in the right room.

Suddenly the huddle breaks. The center is being wiped up and replaced with more sterile green cloths. A stool is pulled up to the operating table . . . *there's my cue.*

One of the praying mantises, still chewing, beckons for me with his prayer appendages. My stomach gurgles with more intensity. The camera! The flash unit! The sync cord! Gotta be careful they don't fumble on anything sterile. The surgical team watches with laser-sharp stares. The swivel stool. Get up on it. Wait wait wait! Check to be sure the seat's twirled all the way down and locked tight. Now get up and focus the camera. Bending over the sterile field under a hot and sinister lamp, my neck begins to break out in sweat. A fleeting thought of this scenario as a futuristic Frankenstein lab zips through my mind. Index finger on the shutter release button and hold your breath . . . *the heart, the pulsing center of the huddle. The praying mantis is chewing in big chomps now. Must've nabbed a big one . . .* Oh my God! What kind of photographs does he want? A macro, normal, or wide-angle shot? Color or black and white? How many of each view? What region of the heart? . . . *looking down the mine shaft I see the raw jewel in the wall. Grotesque with red arteries and blue veins squeezing, letting go, contracting, expanding—like a skilled drummer who never loses the tempo. I'm in awe of its power over life. My heart is beating hard and irregularly. It pounds against the rib cage as if wanting to get out. Uh! It skips a beat!* . . . I spurt out, "Doctor—um, I'm deaf! I have to lipread you and your mask is in the way. Please pull it down for a minute and tell me what you need."

A vigorous jerk sideways registers negative. He points, still gnawing on his prey, to the chest cavity on the table . . . *the heart, exposed to a foreign world of aliens, piercing lights, and cold stainless steel.* "Hurry, do something," *I can feel the heart say.* "You wouldn't like it if someone forced your head under water for a long time!" . . . . The anesthesiologist hurriedly walks to another room and returns with a legal pad and pen. Scribbling on the pad he interprets for the doctor, "How can you possibly handle a job like this?? Never mind—I need a shot of the entire heart and a closeup of the coronary artery. I want two color slides of each view."

Nodding affirmatively and making mental exposure calculations, I climb onto the stool again. All is under control now. Focus. Expose. Advance. Shoot some with lighter exposures and some darker ones. Shoot the entire roll for insurance against Murphy's law.

Anesthesiologist writes, "That'll be all. Send the slides to the doctor after they're processed." A great sigh of relief and suddenly I feel completely drained. My back burns as I step down and feel the hot stares follow me out the door. I make a mental note to thank the anesthesiologist. Somehow. 10:58 a.m.

In the locker room I peel off my wet, green alien skin and toss it in the laundry bin. Turning on the shower and adjusting it to lukewarm, I step in still amazed at how it all happened so fast. I begin to worry if I focused the pictures sharply enough. Were the exposures correct? Was the flash output bright enough? Gotta think of a foolproof way to prevent this from happening again.

I turn off the shower, step out to dry myself, and then put on my street clothes. As I straighten up after tying my shoelaces, my gaze falls on a heart-shaped sticker with a smiling face stuck on one of the lockers. It's the sticker that the blood bank gives out to blood donors. And it says, "I gave blood today!"

I pick up my equipment, head toward the door, and I—smile.

Winter/Spring 1989

Characters in El Paso

Max's friend Lukas straddles a rusted swivel stool at the counter of the Happy Jalapeño, a local café almost within spitting distance of the Rio Grande. It's 7:30 in the morning and the Mexican waitress keeps coming back to give them a written report on their stock:

"We out of green salsa."

"Chorizo sausage comming this afternoon."

"Sorry, no more blue torteeyas today—only yello."

Lukas doesn't utter a word, not even writing a response on the waitress's check pad. Instead, he replies calmly in his most eloquent use of American Sign Language, "You illiterate fry-face, I've come all this way from Tokyo for some Tex-Mex food and now you've picked today to run out of it. Is an American running this place or what?" The smoke overhead from his cigarette creates a sense of fuming anger.

The waitress writes, "Sorry, I not know hand language."

Max reaches over to take her pad and scribble, "Two breakfast burritos—lots of cumin and cilantro. Bring out a bottle of Tabasco." He turns to Lukas: "It'll be as close to Tex-Mex as they can get."

Lukas gestures to the waitress as she's about to turn toward the kitchen.

"Two—coffees." He mimes holding a saucer and sipping from a cup.

"Sí, I know that one!" the waitress says with a smile.

Professor Lukas Volmont is a tall, slender man with a voracious appetite that defies all natural laws of weight gain in a man of sixty-five. Language and literature had been his calling for fifteen years in Washington, DC, at Gallaudet, the world's only liberal arts university for deaf and hard of hearing students, where he pushed them to rise above American Sign Language, their native language (but not leave it behind). He packed Chaucer, Shakespeare, and Chekhov into their isolated deaf-world brains. He couldn't care less if they never learned to speak a word of English, Spanish, or whatever. To survive in this country, they had to be able to read and write in a language other than their own (which couldn't be written on paper anyway).

His favorite phrase was "Read, read, till your eyes bleed." Read everything you see, anything you can get your hands on, even if you have no reading material with you—in this country, there is always something to read in English in your present environment. Read the writing in bathroom stalls, the contents label of your can of drink, your candy wrapper, your cigarette packet, the subway advertisements, bus stop posters, the tags on your underwear. If it contains letters of the English alphabet—read it!

Lukas gave up on them years ago, realizing that his efforts were fruitless except for the occasional attentive student like Max—or so he'd like to think—who tries to absorb everything around him. Lukas also gave up on capitalistic, egocentric, audiocentric America, and tells people that he "deafected" to Japan—typical Lukas fooling with language like that. Actually, he was invited by the Japanese Theatre of the Deaf to go on an international tour with them as a guest artist performing the role of a white professor in their nonverbal visual adaptation of *Kaspar Hauser*. Japan's beauty, economy of space and materials, and its Zen aesthetics lured him to stick around. Max has kept in touch with him throughout the years since his graduation. Lukas is one of the most intelligent deaf role models he has ever met. With no access to any in his line of work, Max puts a premium on any time he can get with Luke. It doesn't help that Max hasn't had a visitor for about a month who was deaf or knew sign language.

Oh, do the Japanese deaf adore him! How many non-Asian deaf people actually study Japanese? They've implored that he stay on with their theatre. Now he is spending his remaining years as a professional actor and lecturer on tour, not in it merely for the acting and adulation but for the education of the masses. Hearing people worldwide need to see that deaf people lead normal lives and that they could even be artists on the stage. He's quite proud of the fact that he's the oldest working deaf actor on Earth.

"Theatre is the best teacher of life" is one of his oft-repeated proverbs. Max had his doubts, though. Lukas always wears secondhand clothing and orders the cheapest fare on the menu. How come he never learned to prosper beyond used clothing and second-rate food?

"What are you reading these days?" Lukas signs.

127

"Not much, a Patricia Cornwell paperback here and there—but mostly technical manuals on biomedical photography."

"Ah, studying diseased-dead flesh."

"I'm killing myself in the photo lab working and studying fifteen hours a day. I'm on a medical-legal photography rotation here for a few weeks. Not much time for pleasure reading."

With half-framed reading glasses worn near the edge of his hawk nose, Lukas glances over some Japanese writings from a hardcover book propped up by a napkin dispenser. Several napkins are filled with doodlings of Japanese characters as he tries to memorize the precise strokes and structures of various ideograms. Japanese is his sixth language.

The waitress sets down their coffee and scoops out a handful of creamer cups from her apron pocket. She gestures coffee to Max as if he didn't know what the creamers were for.

"Shame." Lukas put his pen down and looks at Max. "You're going to spend the rest of your life working inside darkrooms and morgues? Very macabre."

"Of course not," Max said. "I'll get to work in a medical school environment . . . that's pretty prestigious in itself. And, usually with the country's leading researchers and doctors. Like right now I'm working with the one of the nation's foremost forensic pathologists! He's like that TV doctor, 'Quincy M.E.' He removes bullets and foreign objects from bodies, and I take the closeup photos that help him with medical-legal cases in court. I get my photos published alongside his articles in pathology journals and textbooks. He really likes my work. Says I know how to make photographs really sharp with just the right exposure and contrast—better than the other guys." Max decides not to mention that the pathologist works in the morgue with Tubesock, a stinky pet ferret that mostly hangs out on one of his shoulders.

Lukas nods his head and pulls out a fresh napkin from the dispenser. The waitress brings their meal to the counter.

"Food," she gestures, hand-to-mouth, feeling a little more confident with them.

Lukas looks at Max and then at her. Max intercepts Lukas's raised hand, knowing he is about to sign something inappropriate.

Max gives her a "thumbs-up" approval, and then she leaves with jubilant purpose in her step.

At a table behind Lukas sits a heavyset man smoking filterless cigarettes. His bulk covers most of his belt. The man repeatedly spits bits of tobacco from his yellowish-brown tongue. Several pieces get caught on his stomach, missing the floor. His greasy gray hair has a copper tint near where it parts on the left. Between sips of coffee and puffs of smoke, his face pinches from hacking so hard.

"You know, Lukas, just down the street there they even let me go into the OR to photograph operations," Max signs, hoping he might think this is more prestigious and impressive. "Imagine them letting a deaf person in the sacred world of the OR?"

"Why wouldn't they? You're a very capable intern learning the tools of the trade."

"Yeah, but the communication issue. The doctors in the OR all wear masks and hats covering most of their faces. It's completely sterile in there—they can't remove their masks."

"So?" Lukas sketches some new Japanese strokes on the napkin. When he looks up, Max continues.

"How do you expect me to lipread them?"

"I don't. I expect you to write back and forth with them," signs Lukas.

"That's exactly what I do. I always bring a pad and paper with me into the OR. Sometimes even the OR nurses help with the written communication."

"Elementary," signs Lukas.

"What was that about elementary school?"

"I didn't say anything about school. I said 'E-l-e-m-e-n-t-a-r-y'," Lukas fingerspells, as if emphasizing the letters with the bold clarity of alphabet blocks.

At a nearby table, a young mother tries to feed her son. The little boy twists around in his high chair and babbles to the heavyset man. The mother coaxes the boy to eat a forkful of scrambled eggs. He opens his mouth, takes what he can, but doesn't turn toward her. Lumps of egg fall to the floor like pieces of an old yellow sponge. The boy reaches out toward the man, stretching the limits of his high chair belt. He squeals. The man lights another cigarette and coughs. The boy laughs. When the man talks to him, only his gums and tongue show. Not having any teeth seems to make it easier for him to converse in the little boy's language. They could talk back and forth all day long—a conversation across the ages.

Lukas lights up another cigarette after eating his breakfast burrito. He turns a page in his book and peels a fresh napkin from the dispenser.

The man starts to babble and hack constantly, not giving the kid a chance to interject. The conversation overlaps now with neither listening to the other. The mother loads up another forkful of eggs, except this time laces it with ketchup. Her son backhands the fork. The man quickly turns his head in the direction of the blood-like splats he hears land on the floor.

Max finishes his burrito and swivels on the stool to face directly at Lukas. Lukas looks sideways at him, putting down his felt pen. The pen bleeds black onto the napkin.

"Hey who's your buddy over there?" Max says.

"Who?"

"That guy behind you."

Lukas swivels around and sees the man.

"Oh, him."

Max is playing Lukas's game here. Whenever they get together in restaurants while he's back in the States, he'll ask Max things like, "Who's your new girlfriend?" thumbing at a homely woman eating alone at a table. Max would give a wan smile and say, "Yeah, yeah, go on back to your dressing room where you belong." Just to break the boredom of being on international theatre tours, Lukas would go up to the woman and in sign language say, "He loooooooves you." No one would need an interpreter to translate what Lukas signs. Any idiot would understand the way Lukas simply points at Max, crosses both hands over his heart showing the well-known sign for "love," and points at the woman. Most of the time, people are dumbfounded and speechless at Lukas's brash behavior.

"Hey, Luke, why don't you go on over and talk literature with him?" Max says, pointing at the man.

"I'll need an interpreter." Lukas takes a long drag on his cigarette, squinting his eyes to shield the smoke.

"Hell, you never need one when you write back and forth with pretty women in bars."

"He can't read." Lukas takes off his glasses and slides them neatly into a leather-bound case with the poise of an actor being filmed up close, very aware of his screen presence and effect on an audience.

"Uh-huh! You're pretty sure of yourself, huh?"

"Yes, I know he can't," Lukas signs.

"C'mon, you've never met him! How do you know?"

Lukas stands up and combs his wiry gray hair back with his fingers. He counts out a handful of coins and leaves a small stack on the counter, collects his napkins, and slips them into his book as a bookmark.

Lukas looks at Max, and signs, "Elementary. Look at his eyes." He gives Max a hug and an unexpected peck on his forehead. As he passes the man's table, Lukas pulls out one of his doodled napkins, leaves it on the table, and walks out of the restaurant.

Outside looking in through the plate glass window, Lukas signs: "I'll write you . . . maybe in Japanese." He winks. "Sayonara!"

Max gets his attention before he crosses Paisano Drive to walk along the river back to his hotel.

"Hey, Luke! You know where you are?"

He looks at Max with professorial condescension. He sighs. "The Pass of the North."

Max gives him a puzzled expression.

"1581. The first Europeans passed through here. Before that, Indians traveled by for millennia. Long before the Mexicans claimed it as theirs."

"You lost me," Max says.

"It's all right there in that pile of brochures by the door in there," he signs. "If you ever take the time to read."

"No, I meant, do you know the sign for this city?"

"El Paso," Lukas signs, his right "L" handshape moving past his other hand shaped in an "O."

"Do you know why that's the sign for it?"

Lukas shakes his head.

"L pass O—get it?" Max winks back. Lukas gives him an "okay" gesture in sarcastic approval. Watching him walk away in that long gait of his, smoke trailing behind, Max wonders how long it will be till he sees him next. Would Max still be in Texas? Would he get a medical photo job somewhere in the University of Texas system after his rotation was up? He hopes it will be Galveston.

The heavyset man senses something has been put in front of him. He feels around the table until his fingers discover the shape and embossed texture of the napkin. His eyes look up at the ceiling. They move in rapid little circles trying to decode this familiar yet foreign object that Lukas laid before him.

The mother and her son have left. Max picks up his tab and pays the waitress. She motions to wait while she writes something on her check pad. He checks his watch and looks out the window at the towering exterior walls of the university done in Dzong, a distinctive type of architecture popular with Buddhist temples in the Himalayas.

The waitress shows Max what she wrote:

"How you do goodbye?"

Max waves his hand, as in the universal "bye-bye."

She giggles and copies him. "Bye-bye."

As Max leaves, he notices with a start that the man with gray eyes has no pupils. The man holds the napkin up to his nose and sniffs both sides. He rubs the napkin between his fingers, searching, unaware that the mystery is Professor Lukas Volmont's Japanese characters.

2012

The Seawall

Reynaldo slowly sat up in the backseat of the Gran Torino, yawned, and then bunched up his sleeping bag over his brand-new portable tape deck. He crawled over to the front seat. His foot knocked out the plastic dome light cover as he felt around for loose change underneath the litter on the floor. He found a dollar's worth of coins and got out of the car.

Inside the 7-Eleven, he went to the refrigerator where single cans were stored and got out a tall can of Budweiser. He spilled his change onto the counter where the clerk carefully counted each grimy coin. Reynaldo hurried back to the car and took out a disposable pack of salt and his plastic container of reconstituted lemon juice from the glove compartment. After he filled the brim of his beer can with lemon juice and salt, he started up the car and headed for the hospital.

On the east end of the island, the monolithic structure of the University of Texas Medical Branch was lit with yellow spotlights. Preparation for emergency surgery was underway on the fourth floor in OR #2 for a burn victim brought in from an offshore oil explosion. A medical photographer, on twenty-four-hour call, had been paged to photograph the burns on the patient's body for insurance purposes. The photographer leaned against the wall waiting for the nurses to cut away the work clothes. The patient, in shock and under heavy sedation, sat on the stretcher and stared at the change in his body. The doctors stood with folded arms around a draped table readied with surgical tools. One whispered something into the ear of the other. They laughed under the cover of their face masks. The photographer yawned and looked at his watch, then looked around for a stool to sit on.

A nurse came into the room and said something to the circulating nurse. Both looked over at the photographer while they talked. The nurse left and the circulating nurse came over. She wrote something in pen on her scrub pants for the photographer. He read the message on her thigh and nodded, gesturing "okay" with his fingers. He looked at the burn patient and went out the door, leaving his camera equipment on a small table.

Reynaldo was waiting by the receptionist's window outside the sterile core of operating rooms. The photographer stopped halfway down the hall when he saw who was by the window. He shook his head and then proceeded. Reynaldo gave him a big smile and waved hello.

"You're not supposed to see me in this area," said the photographer.

"You told me okay visit you hospital here," Reynaldo said.

"No, only in the photo lab—in the basement, I said. Remember? How did you find me here?"

"Other photographer told me. Me finish visit basement, you not there. He told me you here. Me need talk with you."

"I'm not supposed to be talking here. I could get fired. Now you go. We'll talk later."

The photographer grabbed Reynaldo by the arm and pulled him over by the wall to make way for an orderly pushing a draped body on a gurney.

"He dead?" asked Reynaldo. "What happened?"

"Yes. Now, go on."

"Every day, you see-see that?"

"Yes, but we shouldn't be talking here. Now go. I gotta go back and take pictures."

"Meet lab later?"

"No, I prefer outside of the hospital. We talk too much at the lab. It's not good," the man said.

The receptionist stared over her computer terminal at the two men arguing with their hands. She motioned to another to wheel her chair over for a look.

"Why?" asked Reynaldo.

"Makes me look like I'm socializing all the time at work. Please, I'll meet you later. Just tell me where, I'll show up, okay?"

"Meet restaurant, near wall. Know where?"

"The seawall's ninety blocks long. How am I supposed to know?" asked the man.

"You know, red, blue lights, pretty. H . . . something."

"Yeah, yeah, I know. Go on. See you later. My beeper is vibrating, I gotta get back," the man said.

The Seawall

The street light glare along the seawall boulevard gave the breaking surf a bile-like color. Offshore, oil rigs outlined with beacons continued to pump through the night. Cars and people drifted by slowly through the humidity. The only bright spot was the blinking neon sign, "HOLLYWOOD CAFE," that hung behind the salt-misted window. Near the window, the man stared across the red Formica table at Reynaldo.

"Why did you steal it?" the man asked. He was chewing on his mustache.

"My son," said Reynaldo.

"But your son is too young to want one. Besides, he probably won't have any use for it until he gets older."

"I want sell, get money."

"What do you need the money for? Reynaldo, look at me."

Reynaldo rolled the saltshaker between his palms, a Gerber baby food jar with ice pick holes poked through the lids. The baby's smiling face on the label was almost gone.

"I want buy son hot dog," said Reynaldo.

"A hot dog?"

"On seawall, Saturday."

"I could've given you money for that, Rey. You know I would. I gave you my good pants, didn't I?"

A waitress with crossed eyes came over to take their order. The man couldn't tell if she was looking at him or Reynaldo. He went ahead and wrote on his napkin, asking for their list of Mexican beers. She shook her head and pointed to a Budweiser sign.

"They only got Bud here?" the man asked Reynaldo.

"Here cheap," said Reynaldo.

The man gave the waitress an "okay" gesture.

"I can't believe it—no Tecate?" the man asked. This is a Mexican joint, am I right?"

"Yeah."

"You come here a lot?"

"Fridays. Free coffee."

The waitress returned with two tall cans of beer with pieces of ice melting on the rims. The man looked around at the customers. A couple of men at the counter near the window stared listlessly into

135

the holes of their beer cans. A fat couple at the other end were petting and necking with each other. In the corner booth, a dark, emaciated old man coughed hard. Bits of food shot out of his mouth.

"Your pants. Broken," said Reynaldo. He toyed at a piece of ice with his tongue.

"You broke my pants?"

"Zipper."

"Aw, I don't care. Reynaldo . . . Reynaldo, look at me."

"You disappointed . . . me?" he asked.

"Well, no . . . yeah, yes. Look at me. That doesn't mean I'm going to stop being your friend. What's your sign down in Mexico for friend? I forget."

"Amigo," he said.

"Yeah, that's it. Amigo. You and me, amigos. But if you get caught, I won't have the bucks to bail you out."

The man slapped at a mosquito and flicked it off his arm.

"You photographer," said Reynaldo.

"That doesn't make me rich. And it doesn't mean you can feel free to steal tape decks or whatever from K-Mart 'cause your amigo can save you every time."

"You take beautiful skilled pictures."

"So?"

"Many dollars in your pocket."

"Uh-uh, I'm barely getting by. Hospital pays me like a janitor. Nobody's buying my freelance work, and you know what? Rey . . . I hate it when you look away. What're you looking at?"

"Poor man there."

The dark man in the corner picked up a plastic wrapper off the floor and used it to cover his hand to eat his roll. He slid on three pats of butter, took a bite, and washed it down with a swig from his can of Budweiser. Beer dribbled down his chin. He coughed again, spraying bits of bread. When he finished his roll, he crumpled up the wrapper and threw it back where it came from. He hawked a wad of phlegm and spat it under the table.

"I'm still paying off my camera equipment, my bicycle, TV, and, on top of that, rent and food."

"You rich."

"Come off it, I'm not rich. Now, where's the tape deck—in your car?"

"Yeah. In sleep bag."

"Are you sleeping in your car again? Don't tell me . . . you can't pay for your room anymore."

Reynaldo picked out dirt from under his fingernails with a fork.

"Look . . .your wife's family can't do this to you," said the man.

"See son two hours, Saturdays now."

"They cut down your visiting hours?"

"Told me court order."

"They're liars!"

"I good father . . . bring flowers for wife, tell her I love her. She not understand—mental problems, you know. Her mother, brother, sister protect her. They ask me, 'Where money? Where money?'"

"Do you give them all your money?"

"Mother take . . . for the boy."

"Do you give them all your money every Saturday?"

"Yeah."

"You work your ass off at the tackle factory; you clean the movie theater every night, and then give your paychecks to that woman?"

"I want see my boy."

"Hide some of it. They won't know."

"They know. I don't care money. Son want see me bad. I deaf, he deaf—we same. I make son laugh."

Reynaldo rolled the pepper shaker, which still had its label intact. He stared at the baby's picture. The man looked at the black velvet pictures of valiant toreadors hanging crooked on the wall.

"Reynaldo . . . I'm leaving here for good next week. I've got to get off this island."

"What wrong? Don't like here?"

"Nothing. I like Galveston. I like drinking beers with you in the movies . . . ."

"Where you go?"

"California."

"California have Tecate, lime, salt?

"Yes."

"Can I go with?"

137

"You can't."

"Why? You, me amigo. Live together, eat together, lie in sun together—"

"NO! I'm sorry. I must go . . . alone."

The man paid for the beers and handed Reynaldo a fifty dollar bill. He gave Reynaldo a quick hug and then hurried out the door. He stopped to look both ways before he crossed the boulevard to get to the seawall. Fifteen feet below, the man watched the murky water swish garbage around the boulders. He started to walk west but stopped and looked back. Reynaldo was still at the table playing with the Gerber baby food jars.

1993

A Dive for Home

Every time I looked at my duffel, I thought of my father being carried in a black body bag through an aisle of waist-high piles of *Sporting News* and *Sports Illustrated* in the living room and across his front porch to the coroner's wagon. If Pop could have his way in the after-world, he'd unzip that bag, stick his head out laughing, and say, "So long, Rip! I'll be watching the games from a bird's-eye view. Pitch me some no-hitters, hear?" He'd wink at me and grab the zipper, and say, "Ok boys, off to the showers." His hand would disappear as the zipper closed over him.

The bus driver locked the luggage compartment under the bus and dumped the duffel bag on the highway shoulder near my feet. He tapped me on the shoulder and motioned for me to watch. I put a pinch of snuff down against my gums in front of my teeth. The driver's squat fingers wrapped around an imaginary baseball bat. He pounded the bat once on a crushed milk carton on the ground and went into a batter's stance. He swung at an invisible ball and then shielded his eyes as he saw his ball travel far in the direction where the highway met the horizon. I rolled my eyes in case anyone was looking down through the windows at me next to the driver's goofy baseball pantomime. It was embarrassing enough to inform him that I was deaf and on my way to baseball training when I boarded back in Fort Wayne, Indiana. I took a side glance at the windows to see if people were watching this dumb show. If anyone was taking pity on me, I was thankful not to see it, because the windows reflected just the blue sky and clouds.

I spat out a wad of tobacco juice just before the driver gave me a hearty slap on the back and a thumbs-up gesture. He climbed aboard and wheeled the bus away in the direction of his "home run."

I picked up my duffel and looked both ways before crossing Route 13. It wasn't necessary; the bus was the only moving vehicle around for miles. Directly across the highway was the motel, and through the gray diesel fumes I tried to guess which room would be my new home.

Across the motel's expansive brown lawn, I shuffled my boots to stir up dirt. I missed seeing the infield dust of a baseball field. It had been two weeks since Pop died. When I got the call, I put Pop's affairs in order as quickly as I could so I could make it to the Bluefield Orioles baseball training camp—only got one shot at making it in this farm league before trying to work my way up to the pros in Baltimore.

I stumbled across a square slab of cracked concrete hidden by overgrown grass. It was obviously a heliport with a faded "H" painted inside of a large yellow circle. The blue landing lights were broken at each corner. One corner had a fire extinguisher in a glassless case. A tall wooden pole with a frayed windsock at the top stood at another corner. I looked around for a clue to why there was a helipad on the motel's front lawn. All I saw were corn fields that stretched out for miles with chicken farms and farmhouses planted every half mile or so—no sign of the Bluefield Orioles farm league training complex or anyone.

Pop would have been surprised that I made it in the minor leagues. He gave up on me when I barely escaped getting cut from my high school's junior varsity team.

"Whaddya mean, you made jay-vee? That's for little league losers."

"But Pop, it's a start. I'll work my way up to varsity in no time."

"Waste-a-time . . . them varsity coaches just keepin' you on jay-vee to satisfy high school quota, that's all."

"What quota?"

"Oh, those schools all got some kinda rule 'bout keepin' enough players on varsity and jay-vee so's they can get public funds ever' year. You're just keepin' the benches smooth for them, boy." That last statement kept me chewing away at this sport to this day.

Spring training was scheduled to start next Monday. The rest of the Bluefielders were supposed to be in by Sunday, a week from today. I left a little early because I could no longer stand the empty air of my father's house. Besides, I wanted some time on my own to get up to speed with my running and throwing . . . to be in training before training even began.

"Let me tell ya something, boy," my father once told me before Little League season began, "all them other pitchers got paper for fingernails. If we can get your fingernails as hard as the nails I hammer boards with, you're on your way to baseball Hall-a-Fame. You'd a make me one proud father."

It was then that he started me on this five-year diet of Jell-O. I had to eat a large bowl of it every night after supper although for the longest time I couldn't understand why.

"Just eat it, it's good for you," he'd say. I got used to it as it got me out of eating lima beans and spinach and such. That was our trade-off: greens for yellows and reds. Every week he looked at my fingernails under a light and chewed on one of them to check for toughness.

"Dad, what are you doing that for?"

"Seeing if the Jella's working right."

"How can something so floppy make my fingernails hard?"

"Boy, you ask too many comp-cated questions. Trust me."

I looked around the motel property for a place where I could start practice throwing my knuckleballs. Actually "suckerballs," my father called them, because of the way ballplayers swung at them and missed with "SUCKER" written all over their faces. I was going to have to stand a week of not having a ball thrown back to me. Pop would bite my head off if he thought I was whining about that. I spat out another wad of tobacco juice.

Something moved in the corner of my eye. I turned around and saw several "For Sale" signs sway in the wind in front of deserted mobile homes on a parking lot next to the motel. All of their windows were shut with the blinds drawn. None of them had an outside ledge, which reminded me of the time my father took me outside our home next to one of the front windows. This was after six months of his weekly examinations of biting and chewing a piece of my fingernails.

"Hold your arms up. Keep your fingers out," he said.

"What're you doing?"

"Just do as I say," he said, and gave me a whack upside my head. "Hold 'em up." He picked me up and told me to hang onto the windowsill. And there I was, hanging by my fingernails for all the world to see.

"Stay that way for a while," my father said. "It's the only way you're gonna be able to throw them suckerballs."

Sure enough, in my first year in Little League, I won the MVP award at the All-Star game in my town of Fort Wayne. I was the only pitcher around who could throw a knuckleball. The key to knuckleballs was "not the knuckles but the fingernails," Pop preached. "Yours are hard as nails now. You'll be gunnin' to be the next Phil Niekro."

"Who's that?" I asked.

"You dunno who dat is?? Niekro threw 3,342 strikeouts. Why, he's the winningest knuckleballer in baseball history!"

I rapped my knuckles on the motel's registration desk. Behind it on the wall was a large, curled poster calendar of the Taj Mahal with the year 1988 on it. No one was around, but I smelled incense and burned coffee. Next to the register was a handmade card, "Welcome to Sunny Acres" drawn in a childish way with flowers around the border. Along the Masonite walls were blue-tinted color photographs of a white, heavyset, bald-headed man in aviator sunglasses standing next to a Bell helicopter with its huge soap-bubble cockpit. He looked just like Pop. It seemed that once men became fat, bald, and gray, they took on this common look as if they were part of some national brotherhood. I knocked a few more times. I never knew if those little motel bells really worked, so I gave this one a ring as well. A plump woman in a yellow sari appeared from behind a tapestry divider. The flickering glow from a television bounced off the ceiling above the tapestry.

I pointed to my ears to show that I couldn't hear. I took out a scratch pad from my back pocket and wrote, "Isn't this supposed to be the Route 13 Inn?"

She looked at me and shook her head twice, sort of sideways. Great! Miles out in the middle of nowhere and I was at the wrong place—even she looked like she was at the wrong place. I pointed to the Sunny Acres card and gave her a questioning look. She tilted her head twice again.

"Where's the Route 13 Inn?" I scribbled.

She pointed to "Sunny Acres" on the card. I jabbed the pen at the question on my pad, thinking, "I know this is Sunny Acres, idiot, but where's the Route 13 Inn?"

She tapped at the card, probably figuring that I'm not only deaf but dumb too. I showed her my travel itinerary. Her index finger pointed to the itinerary and then to the card. I pointed to the card and back to the itinerary, putting on another questioning expression. Her head bounced two times to the side. No again? I put my pen in her hand and pushed the scratch pad toward her.

"We the new owners," she wrote. "We name here Sunny Acres." She smiled and pushed the registration clipboard to me. At last, we were communicating. I printed my father's name, Bill Ripley. It was mine also, another one of those things that made me think of him.

I unlocked the door to Room 5, trying to figure out why the woman shook her head in that odd, slanted way. Inside, the air smelled years old. I propped the door open with the duffel bag. I jumped on the bed and leaned over to the curtain rod to separate the pair of green and white checkered curtains. The view of the empty pool looked better than the curtains.

I padded over to the other side of the bed to turn on the ceiling fan, which seemed to be the room's best feature. In the bathroom, I turned on the faucet, which sputtered brown water into my hands. I let the water run a while to clear itself and get rid of the sulfur smell . . . also to wash away the leftover snuff I spat into the sink.

I moved a recliner close to the middle of the room under the fan and plopped down onto it. My whole body felt heavy. I didn't want to think about baseball or what to do with Pop's house. I lived there all eighteen years of my life, the last two without my mother, who passed on. For two years after Mom died, Pop became a hoarder—probably his way of grieving. In his mind, the more junk he gained, the less he'd have to deal with the loss.

Outside, I saw that the milkweeds were interwoven with the diamond-shaped wiring of the pool fence. I pushed the chair back to let my body get more air from the fan. The motel's a dive, I thought, but I'm glad it's got that ceiling fan . . . really . . . a nice, old-fashioned fan . . . I'm happy the fans are here . . . very nice . . . happy fans . . . waving fans . . . .

Then I slipped into this recurring dream of being chased by a tornado, except this time it's on a baseball field and I'm a base runner taking a big lead off of first base. I wanted to get to home plate but the tornado funneled to the ground just beyond center field.

I saw Pop in the stands mouthing the words, "Go Rip, go! Go Rip, go! Go Rip, go!" Like a sharp pitcher, the tornado caught me off guard with a smokescreen of dirt. In a panic, I made the split-second decision to dart toward where I hoped was home plate. I ignored all the rules of base running and didn't round second and third but headed straight for home. As I ran, I felt suction on my back. I heard a loud approaching roar, a weird sensation since in real life I couldn't hear such things. As I almost touched home plate, I couldn't resist the temptation to look back. What I saw was a large windpipe with ribbed walls that hollered into infinity. It was then that I looked forward to home plate and took the flying leap.

I didn't know how long I was out, but the last thing I remembered was screaming the word "safe." My knuckles were pale from clutching the recliner arms and I saw that my feet were still pointed from the dive I took in my dream. The fan with its toothy grin and wide, rotating blades breathed lazy, lukewarm air in my face.

When I leaned forward the back of my shirt peeled off the chair's vinyl covering; I smelled stale cigarettes swoosh out between the seams of the seat foam. The odor conjured images of people that stayed here—drippy drunks who smoked voraciously, prostitutes who exhaled smoky veils to conceal a dead tooth or a scar from a trick, lonely salesmen who blew away boredom by watching smoke rings get chopped up by the fan.

Through the picture window, the battered "swim at your own risk" sign waved back and forth, its corner hanging by a hook on the fence. The short diving platform still needed someone to put the board back on.

My shirt felt a little dry now. I wanted to get up to do some warm-ups outside, but I sank back in the chair, still exhausted from the long trip. A light wind blew through the bathroom window and swirled dust balls around the linoleum floor. Brown water still ran from the faucet. On the dresser were paper cups and bright blue-and-white boxes of lemon-flavored Jell-O unpacked from my duffel bag. I looked up at the ceiling fan and stared.

The rotor of a helicopter began to rotate.

My father's bald head lolled in the body bag.

The magazine piles toppled over.

My eyelids grew heavy.

The air became still, and somehow . . .

. . . far away, I heard a roar.

September 2021

The Ear

Jessie Sweetwind was out on a five-mile run during a cold twilight evening thinking about her deaf students when she almost stepped on an ear. What caught her eye—and helped make that split-second decision to avoid stepping on it—was the wetness and color of flesh.

She continued running, freezing the image in her mind as she made her way up to the top of a hill that marked the run's halfway point, where she would turn around a couple of wooden barrier posts and head back. Should she pass the posts and improvise a new route home, or turn around and get a good look at that thing to be sure it wasn't what she thought it was? A half hour of ambient blue light was left before it would become black. There were no lights along the footpath and the moon hadn't risen yet. Around and around the posts Jessie ran doing figure eights.

Eileen should've been with her. She usually accompanied Jessie on these runs, often filling her in on various environmental sounds like the babbling brook, a drilling woodpecker, or coupling teenagers. Mainly, Jessie wanted Eileen for security—she was big-boned, taught phys ed, coached field hockey, and there was no one Jessie would rather have along than a woman who knew how to throw a block or a verbal attack should danger come their way. Eileen enjoyed coming along since she could maintain a steady breathing rhythm, signing while running with Jessie—both conversed in American Sign Language without voice. She especially liked how signing added a bit of aerobic activity for the upper body.

Jessie stopped going around the posts and began running in place facing downhill. Usually, her body was warmed up by now, but she still felt the dull ache of cold in her feet and legs. A month ago while she and Eileen were running side by side, Eileen heard a gunshot and immediately shoved Jessie on the ground not far from where the ear was. Jessie rolled hard down the hill and smacked her head against a tree stump alongside the pathway. Before she realized what Eileen had done, blood streamed down her face, turning her world red. Jessie ended up getting ten stitches in her scalp.

She never saw the source of the gunshot so she had to take Eileen's word for it. Jessie didn't like the eerie power hearing people have over deaf people in situations like this; the same kind of power when they live on both sides of your apartment and hear just about everything you do—grinding your coffee, flushing your toilet, your burps, coughs, and sneezes, all of your private noises—but you can't hear what they do. Jessie knew this because her passive-aggressive neighbor would let her know when she ground her coffee rather early in the morning, or when she had been up all night with a male visitor. The woman had the ears of a cat.

Down below, Jessie could barely see the speck of flesh in the middle of the blacktop. Lined along the path were bare elms with branches reaching out into the night. "What would Eileen do if she were in my Nikes?" Jessie thought. Eileen had called earlier.

"SORRY . . . HAVE TO BACK OUT TODAY . . . GOT A EADACHE, GA," typed Eileen.

As soon as Jessie saw the "GA" symbol for go ahead, she immediately typed back on her TTY, an old Model 28 teletypewriter converted to allow deaf people to communicate with others on the telephone.

"A EADACHE? U MEAN EARACHE, GA?" Sometimes the old clunker hit the wrong letters or missed them entirely, making Jessie play guessing games.

"NO, NO . . . HEADACHE," said Eileen.

"WHAT AM I GONNA DO WITHOUT MY SECRET SERVICE ESCORT? GA," said Jessie.

"I DON'T THINK THAT'S FUNNY, JESS. GA"

"WAS BEING HALF FUNNY. AM SERIOUS, TAKE A COUPLE TYLENOLS. DON'T FEEL COMFORTABLE RUNNING BY MYSELF TODAY. GA"

"NO CAN DO. MUST REST MY POOR HEAD TODAY (FROWN). COULD USE A BREAK FROM EXERCISING," said Eileen. "WHY NOT WEAR UR HEARING AIDS WHILE RUNNING? GA"

"RUIN THEM WITH SWEAT? NO WAY! GA," said Jessie.

"IT'S WINTER—U WON'T SWEAT THAT MUCH. WHY R U RUNNING THIS AFTERNOON ANYWAY? DAY BEFORE

THANKSGIVING—UR THRU WITH TEACHING FOR THE AFTERNOON. TAKE A LOAD OFF. (SMILE!) GA" Eileen frequently added words in parentheses to reflect her facial expression at the moment, since tone of voice gets lost through the TTY. Jessie despised them; it made her feel she had no imagination, but she couldn't tell Eileen that. After all, Eileen showed a lot of effort by purchasing her own TTY and keeping up with issues and trends in the Deaf world.

"THE FACT I'M RUNNING WILL TAKE A LOAD OFF," said Jessie. She showed her rear end to the TTY. "WELL, UR LOSS . . . XXX . . . I MEAN, UR GAIN. CAN'T LOSE POUNDS STAYING HOME. GA"

"DON'T U WORRY—I'M NOT A CALORIE COUNTER. (SMIRK!) GA"

"HA! U THINK I DO THAT? GO BACK TO UR CHIPS, SALSA, AND SEINFELD. GA OR SK?" Jessie stuck her tongue out at the TTY and whacked the side of it.

Signing off, Eileen typed, "CRUNCH CRUNCH CRUNCH MMMMMM YUMMY YUM, GA TO SK."

Jessie repeatedly hit the signing off symbols hard, the "S" and "K" keys, as if she were poking someone's eyes out. She hung up, and yelled, "Fat bitch!" to the TTY printout. "The third time you've canceled out on me this month." She'd love to know how clearly her neighbor's ears understood her deaf speech.

Almost near the ear on the path, Jessie went into a jog. She had decided to run today anyway to compensate for the upcoming Thanksgiving dinner. When family and friends asked why she ran every day, she said it was to meditate, but the real reason was her obsession with staying thin.

Slowing down, Jessie glanced again at the fleshy object and then picked up speed. When she got to the wooded area past the townhome community, she saw a 7-Eleven paper sack blown against a bush. She thought of the film *Blue Velvet* she recently quizzed her Lit and Film students on. Early in the film was a scene where the main character, a young, wholesome amateur detective, discovered a severed ear in a vacant lot. He found a paper bag and with a stick lifted the ear into the bag and took it to the police station, thereby linking the ear to a dark underworld.

Jessie couldn't believe such a parallel was happening right now. She stopped, resting her hands on her knees, and breathed hard. What if this flesh thing really was evidence to a crime scene? It wouldn't be right to just leave it, unsolved.

She grabbed the 7-Eleven bag and ran uphill to where the hunk of flesh was laid. Or, was it flung there? Cut out from a human being on the spot? A shiver ran up and down her arms. The ear was still attached to the surrounding skin that an ear is typically attached to.

Jessie took a closer look and sniffed. She couldn't smell anything rotten; it sort of smelled like raw chicken. The skin was obviously from a white person. Whatever happened must've happened very recently. On closer inspection she wasn't sure this was an ear. It had the shell-like swirl of an ear but it didn't have a lobe or a curved outer portion; they were snipped off probably with a pair of scissors. Two other diso-rienting items—she didn't see any hair above, in, or around the ear-like object. She couldn't see an opening where there should have been an ear canal—it was getting too dark to tell.

Jessie had the awful feeling that someone criminal was watching her discover his handiwork. She immediately stood up and scanned the area. No one. She looked around for a stick but found a yellow pencil alongside the path. With the pencil's point, she lifted the flesh into the bag. This felt just like the *Blue Velvet* scene, reinforcing a point she made every semester in film class that life sometimes imitated art and vice versa. She surveyed the area once more to be sure no one was looking, and then rolled down the top of the bag.

Feeling that she had evidence to a horrendous crime, she ran hard in the enveloping darkness, switching hands with the bag every quar-ter mile or so. To avoid contaminating the evidence bag, she made a conscious effort not to wipe sweat off her brow.

Getting close to Columbia's town center, she passed a brightly lit lakefront restaurant with people eating steaks and barbecue ribs at the window seats. She imagined the horror in their expressions if the ear soaked through and dropped out of the bag. She smiled.

When Jessie got to her apartment, she put the paper sack outside on top of her woodpile on the back patio. She locked the sliding glass patio doors, closed the blinds, and went to the bathroom to draw a hot bath. Along the tub's edge, she lit some votive candles and piñon incense.

For a half hour she planned her next move while vigorously scrubbing her hands and fingernails. If she called the police, they would probably grill her about why she had this piece of ear, especially considering that she was deaf. Why, they would wonder, would a deaf person of all people pick this thing up way out in the woods two-and-a-half miles away? Then after questioning that, they would size up her body, poke around in the bedroom, look through her bras and panties, open up the medicine cabinet, check out her diaphragm case and sniff it, and squeeze the tube of Ortho creme as if it had some connection with finding the ear. The Rodney King beating and the furor over Mark Fuhrman spoiled her faith in cops.

She held off on the police. Couldn't call her parents—on vacation touring England somewhere. Her sister—already left for Connecticut to visit her in-laws. Didn't want to alarm everyone up there. Her deaf cousin Rachel in New York City, actually her best friend since they're the same age—no one answered except the TTY answering machine. A short message was left wishing Rachel a happy Thanksgiving and to give her a call ASAP. Next, Eileen—same problem, no answer. She couldn't leave a typed message. Eileen had a roommate, and Jessie didn't trust leaving sensitive information on a machine that displayed words for all eyes to see.

The only thing left to do was call her friend Troy, but that would mean having to use the telephone relay service. Relay agents weren't to be trusted. They acted as a third party that relayed TTY calls to hearing people by voice, and converted voice calls into TTY for deaf people. One of them could pick up on her intelligence about the ear and break the code of confidentiality by informing the police.

Jessie was going to leave Columbia soon anyway for Philadelphia, where she would dutifully spend Thanksgiving Day with Troy's family. This was not something to look forward to since Troy and his family were hearing. She'll have to go through the whole tedious routine of lipreading a bunch of numb lips at the dinner table and putting up with Troy's lackluster sign skills. He's known Jessie for three years and still can't sign to save his butt. They were on-and-off-again lovers, which made her suspect his hesitancy to fully commit to learning American Sign Language. At least Troy would be someone to confide in. Maybe he would have a good idea of how to deal with the police, having worked as a security guard for a software company to support himself through law school.

She called him to say she was on her way. The relay agent must have been tone deaf and illiterate for she kept typing "Roy" and "Tessie," and misspelling simple words. When Jessie hung up she gave an "up-yours" gesture at the telephone, partly pissed at the agent and partly to avoid the blame for stupidly accepting a Thanksgiving invite six months ago. She lifted the receiver and banged it back into its cradle for good measure.

Before she left, she brought the paper bag inside. She wiped the bathtub dry and shook the ear out into it. Using eyebrow tweezers, she grabbed the ear and looked at it up close, taking her time turning it over this way and that. It certainly looked like an ear. Underneath the skin were yellow fat globules and dark red muscles that once covered someone's skull. The whole flesh piece was about the size and shape of a kid's baseball glove. The area where a canal was supposed to be bothered her. Perhaps it was a birth defect.

More and more, Jessie felt that in her tub was a crucial piece of forensic evidence that police nationwide must be scrambling all over for. If she handled this right, she could see herself in national news-papers positively portrayed as a model citizen (and a deaf one at that) who broke wide open a major crime. That would knock down all those stereotypes hearing people have of deaf people always needing guid-ance and salvation. Her neighbor would finally see her as an equal and lay the hell off her.

Jessie dropped the ear into the bag and set it inside an opening in her woodpile. The cold would prevent it from rotting.

The overnight stay in Philadelphia was blessedly brief. The lips at the table were as numb and dumb as ever. Troy was the same but the turkey was quite good. By three in the morning, Jessie was back home in her own bed. She kept waking up thinking the police had entered her bedroom. After a trip to the bathroom, she went to the patio door and parted the blinds. The bag was still sitting in the woodpile open-ing. Something startling about that . . . the whole experience felt like an illusion while driving to and from Philly, and yet seeing the crum-pled sack again turned it back into a reality.

Back in bed she recalled Troy coming into his family's guest room at night. He tried to slip into bed with her just when they were finally alone and she wanted to burst out her secret finding.

"No, I'm not sleeping with you in your parents' house. You're crazy!" said Jessie.

"Oh c'mon, they won't hear us."

"How am I to know that? What are your parents doing right now?"

"What do you mean?" said Troy. "They're in bed, of course."

"Is your father snoring? Your mother turning a page in a novel? Are they talking to each other? What?" said Jessie.

Troy looked at her with a raised eyebrow.

"Stop rubbing my leg."

"We'll be quiet like mice." Troy made an unintentional gesture of two mice humping. He was trying to sign "making love softly" but ended up pumping one fist on top of the other.

Jessie winced. She didn't want to be up all night arguing about how he was still so incompetent with her language.

"Please sit up," said Jessie. She sat up against the headboard and drew her knees to her chest. "What are they doing?"

"This is the treatment I get after opening my house and family to you and feeding you a delicious meal?" He was massaging her feet and purposely not looking at her for a reply.

She clamped her feet together to get him to remove his hands. He sat up and cocked an ear in the direction of his parents' bedroom.

She looked hard at his left ear. She zoomed it up so that all she saw was the lobe, the shell-swirl, and the pink skin surrounding the ear canal. The image of the severed ear came to mind and she overlapped it with his to see if it fit.

"They're watching *The Tonight Show*. I hear Leno's voice," said Troy, putting his hand on her shoulder. "Talking about something that—"

"I found an ear."

Troy quickly withdrew his hand. "What?" he said.

"Yesterday. I was running and found an ear on the ground. Brought it home," said Jessie. "I wanted to call the police but I'm afraid of what they'll do with me."

"Where did you find it?"

"Out on the path that goes by that bad neighborhood."

"You don't think that—"

"The ear is kinda pinkish," said Jessie. "At least, I think it is. I can't tell if it's really an ear or not. What should I do? The more I wait, the more the police will suspect me." She filled him in on the episode and her fear of cops.

"I thought I told you not to go running in that area anymore," said Troy. "A lot of crime goes on in that area, you know that. Didn't you learn anything from Eileen protecting you when she heard that gunshot?"

"Protecting? Ha! Sometimes I wonder if she did it for the sport of it," said Jessie. "Nobody was out in those woods."

Troy put his hand up to her head. "How's the scar coming along? Your hair's grown back." He signed "grow" like her hair was a weed.

Jessie got out of bed and started putting her belongings into her overnight bag.

"You're not going home already, are you?" Troy ended his questions by drawing a big question mark in the air, an annoying trait hearing people tend to pick up. Most can't grasp the concept that a questioning facial expression alone denoted a question.

"I'm sorry, I can't sleep. And I don't want to be up all night staring at your mother's country cross-stitchings on the wall."

"But you'll wake my parents leaving this late."

"Doubt it. They're watching *The Tonight Show*, right? Right?? Besides, I'll leave like a mouse." She made a bucktoothed expression and wrinkled her nose.

"But what will I tell them in the morning?" said Troy.

"You're a lawyer. Bullshit your way out of it. If you're really stuck, tell them the cranberry and sauerkraut are doing somersaults in my stomach. Tell your father I'm sorry I won't be able to eat his usual wonderful Western omelet tomorrow morning."

"You've got to call the police as soon as you get back. Get it over with."

She kissed him on the cheek and was gone.

Troy's remark about getting it over with kept repeating itself to the point that she gave up trying to sleep. The sky began to show a tinge of light. Twilight, she thought. Most people wouldn't call it that, though. The light looked exactly the same as if it were in the evening.

Not feeling hungry, she made a fire and sat cross-legged in front of it. Every once in a while she looked out the sliding doors at the bag and then at the phone.

"HOWARD COUNTY POLICE, MAY I HELP U? GA." Each letter was typed slowly. Jessie could tell they hardly got TTY calls.

"THIS IS JESSIE SWEETWIND OF COLUMBIA. I FOUND WHAT LOOKS LIKE A SEVERED EAR WHILE OUT RUNNING THIS A.M." Boy, it's easy to lie on the TTY. "THOUGHT IT MAY BE CRIME EVIDENCE. WANTED U TO KNOW ABOUT IT. GA." Suddenly, she slapped the side of her big old gray TTY. Too late! She realized she could've run back to where she found the ear and simply dumped it. Directing the police to it over the phone would've avoided any confrontation with them. She kicked the stout leg of her machine. The printout advanced to the next line.

"UR ADDRESS, PLS? GA."

"5340 SILVER BROOK WAY. GA."

"WE'LL DISPATCH SOMEONE TO UR PLACE WITHIN THE HR. GA TO SK."

Jessie replaced the receiver, made a gun handshape, and aimed it at the telephone. BAM! She went to the bathtub to give it a good scouring. She took her running clothes out of the hamper, sprinkled some water over them, and threw them on the floor near her bed.

The fire was getting low so she went outside to the woodpile. Before taking a log out, she took out the paper sack and set it on top of the logs for the cops to see in plain view.

Much to Jessie's surprise, there were two police officers at the door who were tall, lean, imposing-looking women, one being African American. She wore abstract, tribal-looking earrings that dangled from her free earlobes—the unattached kind. The white officer had on simple, pearl studs pierced into lobes that were attached.

Jessie felt short and fat in her pajamas and bathrobe. She pointed to the bag outside and opened the sliding doors to let the women through.

The policewomen looked at Jessie sitting by the fire and said something to each other that she couldn't pick up from lipreading. They were probably already suspicious that she hadn't said a word and wasn't staying outside to explain the entire situation to them. If for some quirky reason they decided to arrest her, Jessie thought that the first thing she would go for would be the dangling earrings. Create a distraction by ripping them off the earlobes and making a dash out the sliding doors.

They looked into the bag and dumped the ear onto the concrete. How odd that the ear bounced a few times before landing face down. Heads or tails? Jessie tried hard to suppress a giggle. The white policewoman turned the ear over with a stick and jabbed at it a few times. She held the bag open on the ground and flicked the ear into it with the stick. As she closed it the other officer turned her head sideways and talked to her shoulder. Weird. Why was she talking to her shoulder? When she turned a little, Jessie could see a walkie-talkie mouthpiece fastened to her shoulder. She turned again with her shoulder hiding her lips.

Jessie held her hands out to the fire and rubbed them together. They still felt cold. Her stomach quivered. What was her neighbor thinking hearing these officers' voices and the sliding door going back and forth?

The one policewoman stopped listening and talking to the walkie-talkie and conferred with the other by her ear. Why? They were outside. The door was closed. They knew Jessie was deaf. Both glanced inside toward Jessie.

They opened the bag again. Both looked in and nodded their heads, muttering a few more things to each other while looking through the glass at Jessie. When the officers approached the sliding door, she wondered how these women would read her her rights. Jessie stood up and opened the door to let them in. She stood in the doorway and took a quick look outside to be sure nothing was in the way.

The African American policewoman came over to her. The tribal earrings swayed and sparkled, catching the light in the living room. They were renditions of oblong African masks. How far she had come, Jessie thought. From the beginnings of man, to slavery, the Civil Rights movement, and now a police officer in her own right. Jessie took her hands out of her bathrobe pockets.

The officer took out a notepad to write something. Her fingers were long and slender. Well-manicured. Jessie held her breath.

"It's probably a piece of pig," the woman wrote. "People sometimes have pig roasts for Thanksgiving. A dog, cat, or raccoon most likely carried it off and dropped it where you found it." They thanked Jessie for the call and waved goodbye.

Jessie Sweetwind sat down in front of the fire and looked at the note again: "piece of pig." The fire spat an ember. She kept rereading the phrase. How strange that the woman's handwriting was so sloppy and unfeminine. She was so pretty and had all this power.

2012

The Label

She was in Ames for the opening of a play of hers at Iowa State University. After the show, she was unable to sleep all night because of a rapid heartbeat. She admitted herself to the local hospital. Atrial fibrillation. They had her under twenty-four-hour observation to monitor her heart. She emphasized to the staff who came into her room that she was deaf, and if something needed to be said, please face her and enunciate clearly to make it easy to lipread. Naturally, as in any hospital, there was a high turnaround of staff as various shifts came and went throughout the night. This meant that she had to repeat her instructions to each new staff member who entered the room talking, facing away to where she wasn't able to read lips. She told one of the nurses to please make a note on the chart about her communication needs for the others to read so she wouldn't have to keep repeating herself.

All of them encouraged her to try to relax and get some rest but she couldn't because they put her on a bed with a mattress that automatically inflated and deflated at different locations along her body every twenty minutes to prevent bedsores. It didn't help that her upper left arm was also hooked up to a timed blood pressure cuff that went on and off every fifteen minutes.

A friend stopped by to visit her the next morning and asked if she knew about the note posted on the wall behind her.

"What note?"

"The note taped to the wall behind your bed," she said.

"What does it say?"

"Hearing Impaired (Pt reads lips)."

"Damn! They must've snuck in and put that up while I was off on a quick doze."

She pushed herself up and turned around to look at the handwritten note. It dawned on her that she was a label, and one defined on their terms. She had told them that she was "deaf"—pure and simple— yet they wrote the ambiguous, outdated term "hearing impaired" and stuck it on the wall for all to see in broad daylight.

It reminded her of something she once read about the famous playwright Lorraine Hansberry. When she was born, the hospital wrote "Negro" on her birth certificate. Her parents, asserting their right to designate their child's racial identity, crossed out the hospital's label and wrote the word "Black."

2021

Sifting Dirt

Roger Folter leaned against the park's thick iron fence and crossed his right foot over his left. He was a few yards from the water's edge. In the middle of the Le Brea Tar Pits in Los Angeles was a gray mastodon, stuck in tar; its massive trunk and tusks stabbed the sky in a frozen snarl. A squat pigeon rested on the mammoth's back, and down the sculpted shaggy sides were dried white dribbles of dung. As tar bubbles rose passively to the surface near the statue's legs, Roger envisioned his dirt-filled kitchen sink. The living room scene replayed in his head.

"You preach, still," said his wife Rhondee, standing in front of the anchorwoman on the eleven o'clock TV news.

"Move please; she's talking about Bosnia now," said Roger.

"You preach, still," said Rhondee with stronger hand movements.

Roger leaned forward on the sofa to push her out of the way but she slapped his hand off her hip.

"Hey—can't you wait till this is over? he asked.

"No, me saw you—you correct-correct him. Must stop now."

Roger sank back on the sofa.

"Correcting what?" he asked. He craned his neck to catch the newsclip that flashed on the screen.

"You preach-preach English to him," she said.

Roger felt his gut tighten a little, but he let it go.

The bubbles that bobbed up against the mastodon's leg released an oily film in the water. The pigeon fluttered its wings then settled down again on its haunches. Roger closed his eyes, trying to remember what happened next. He had been watching a closed-captioned newscast, reading fast scrolling lines of text at the bottom of the television screen, when Rhondee stepped in. It was a chore to read the news at a frantic pace especially when the captions were fraught with misspellings, but he kept at it knowing that it would pay off in the long run.

Roger looked around the pit to check on his son. On the other side, Cody skimmed rocks across the water. The pigeon flew away. Roger crossed his left foot over his right and went back to the bubbles.

"I'm teaching English to Cody," said Roger. He emphasized "teach" with his hands, retrieving invisible information from his head and pushing it to an imaginary young boy next to him. "Now move—please?"

"You preach-preach!" The veins on Rhondee's neck and face began to surface.

Roger was proud of the way he preserved his emotions. He was a professional who sold his feelings; that's how actors work. Big emotional outbursts were all right for the stage, but the way Rhondee wasted her anger in their warm, serene living room was beyond him.

"Next year we're enrolling Cody in kindergarten, right?" Roger asked his wife.

"Right," she said. The interrupted lines of captions scrolled behind her.

"With hearing children?" he asked.

"Hearing children," she said with a bitter expression.

"Correct," said Roger. "Cody is hearing—we can't help that—he should be around other hearing children, right?"

Rhondee stared at the little scar on Roger's lower lip.

"And what language will these hearing kids be using?"

"English," said Rhondee. "What's the point?"

"Sign that again," Roger said.

Like a bored sign language student, she clasped one hand weakly over her wrist in a classic British pose.

"English."

"Right! And does Cody know English?"

"He knows enough," she said.

"Bathroom, me finish touch," Roger mimicked. "Me-know, me know. Me-want, me-want. You call that English?"

Her eyes narrowed and her nostrils pinched. The unbuttoned pocket flaps on her blouse seemed to open and close as she took big breaths.

"What's—what's wrong—that?" Her hands trembled. "Before never bother-bother you, me not sit here watch-watch captions, improve my English."

"Nothing's wrong if Cody's signing with us or other deaf people. But if he talks like that to his teachers and classmates, they're going to make fun of him."

"Give him time." Her index finger repeatedly jabbed her wrist-watch. "Cody develop natural deaf language now. Dump two languages on little boy, age-four, can't. Later, English."

"I want to start now before it's too late," he said.

"Not now! First, what? He understand us, must! You, me our language before too late."

"Do you want him to look stupid?"

She hit the palm of her hand with a firm karate chop in front of Roger's face. Roger flinched and thought she was going to slice his nose off.

"Stop!" she said.

The bubbles in the pit burst slowly, one after another. Roger felt something tug on his pants. Cody stretched his little french-fry fingers apart and pressed his thumb against his forehead.

"Daddy!"

"What's up?" Roger grimaced as he rubbed a stiffness in the back of his neck.

"Me hear bird. Talk funny."

"I hear a bird. It talks funny," Roger corrected.

"Can't. Hard," said Cody.

"Try it. You're a smart guy."

"Don't wanna."

"Do you want to go home now?" Roger asked. "I don't need to stay here."

"No, no, don't. Me-want stay," cried Cody.

"Then you try harder."

"I hear bird. It talk funny," said Cody.

"That's better. Was that so hard?"

"Yeah."

"Ok. Where do you see this bird?"

"Not see bird but me can hear—says 'Hel-lo!'" said Cody. He fingerspelled the last word leaving the "O" formed in his hand.

"Oh, c'mon Code, you know birds can't talk."

"Come look-for," said Cody.

160

Roger hitched Cody up onto his shoulders; he smelled his light buttery scent, which came from Rhondee, only hers was sharper. As he walked around the tar pit to a nearby construction site, Cody gave him the signal, with a tap of his boot heel, to let him down. Cody ran up to a mound of excavated dirt and climbed up to the top. He had the look of a miniature cowboy scanning a prairie. Roger sat down at the bottom of the mound and scooped up a handful of moist dirt, slowly letting the finer pieces fall between his fingers. He looked over at the tar pit and studied the expression of rage on the mastodon's face.

In the living room, Rhondee still wouldn't budge from her position in front of the television set.

"Face it," said Roger, "we're living in a hearing world."

"Spittie," she said.

"What did you call me?"

"Spittie—pftht, pftht!"

"I don't need to watch that deaf bullshit," said Roger. "Get out of the way. I'm getting behind on world news, you mind?"

Rhondee stepped back and used the anchorwoman for a demonstration.

"You want act like hearing people, 'talk-talk-talk,' spit fly out your mouth."

"Are you making fun of my work?" asked Roger.

"My life, you mock?" asked Rhondee.

There was a moment of stillness in the room except for the flickering images from the television.

"Me show what you look like on stage with hearing actors." She stood erect, expressionless, one hand over her chest and the other behind her back. She imitated a bad actor's monologue, moving only her mouth in grotesque shapes: "Blah-blah-blah."

Roger took a minute to think while the anchorwoman signed off for a commercial break.

"I thought you supported the idea of me integrating with other hearing people?"

"Too much," Rhondee said.

"What's that supposed to mean?"

"You leave behind sign language, Deaf culture."

161

"I'm including it . . . expanding it. To see how far we can go with our potential."

"Uncle Tom," she said.

"You can't deny we live in a hearing world," said Roger overlapping her remark.

"Uncle T-O-M." Rhondee fingerspelled slow to catch his attention. "Uncle Tom?"

"No, no, no; mistake me," she said. "Uncle Tom for blacks. Me mean Uncle R-O-G."

"What's wrong with you, Rhondee?"

"Everything! Thought me married deaf man."

She stared at him, breathing hard. When he couldn't hold the glare, she backed up and left the room. The anchorwoman returned and continued her cool delivery. He went back to the news and absently read the captions.

A few minutes later, Rhondee returned with her arms full of potted aloes from around the house. Dirt spilled on the floor behind her, some stuck to the sweat on her arms. She dumped the pots upside down and filled the sink with black soil. Roger watched from the corners of his eyes, keeping his head in the direction of the television. She grabbed a bunch of aloes and plucked apart the fleshy, fingerlike leaves one by one. The leaves were piled up on top of the butcher block next to the toaster. For an absurd second Roger imagined her making a salad. She took a fork from the drawer and methodically mashed the juices out of the leaves. When she was finished, the clear liquid oozed over the block and onto the counter.

From the far end of the sofa Roger sat with his mouth hung open. He thought of what he should be feeling, but nothing appropriate registered. Her actions surprised him. There was no cue for her next move. She's going to sneer at him, he anticipated, and sign, "Now you know how me feel!" Instead, his wife walked over to the television, unplugged the wires from the closed-captioning device, and wrapped them around the machine. The television image shrank to a dot where the anchorwoman's lips were and disappeared. Rhondee snatched her keys off the top of the microwave oven and left by the front door with her captioning device under her arm. Roger waited for the vibrations to rock across the hardwood floor when the door slams, but nothing happened. She left the door open.

Roger looked back at the television and saw that his wife left behind her muddy handprints all over the screen. He slowly got up to look in the sink. It smelled like a freshly turned garden. He wondered which two of the leaves were the original ones that Rhondee gave him at the start of their relationship, before it had grown wild and out of proportion. Roger padded down the hall to peek into his son's room. Cody had slept through another argument.

Roger was still looking at the mastodon when Cody jumped on his back and knocked the remaining dirt out of his hands.

"Daddy! Me saw balloon man. He make-make balloon, like this . . . " Cody showed his father how the man blew a long, narrow balloon and twisted it into different shapes.

"Well, let's go buy a balloon. You know what kind of animal you want?"

"Yep!"

"Good. And, let's buy one for your mother. You know what kind of animal she wants?" Roger was thinking that Rhondee probably drove over to her mother's to cool off from the fight.

"Don't know," said Cody. "Have idea—we tell balloon man make-make talking bird."

Roger raised his right hand to correct him but restrained himself. He lifted his left hand and signed, "Okay, and then we'll go over to your grandmother's."

Winter 2002

Toxic Waste

9-2-2018

Brookline, MA

Woke up early this morning to get ahead in line for Toxic Waste Dumping Day. Elizabeth and Jeremiah, the people I work for, want me to get rid of some old paint and turpentine. They left instructions last night on the hallway table outside of the old servant's room in their mansion. I live in this room for free in exchange for being a handyman fifteen hours a week:

- "Dig up leaf mold and spread some around the blueberry shrubs."
- "Clear out junk from the walk-in closet in the third floor bedroom."
- "Sweep out the wine cellar and mop with ammonia."
- "Take chainsaw to the shop—tell them to clean out the motor (Little Jerry put in bad gas)."

I keep a record in my journal of the work I've done and the number of hours put in. At the end of each week, I tear out the list of completed chores and leave them on the hallway table for my employers.

Arrived at the dump at 8:30 and twenty cars are already in front of me. The gates don't open until nine. A woman with a clipboard makes her way down the line of cars. She stops at each vehicle to jot something down. The woman in the car in front of me gets out to pick and eat some roadside berries.

Knew I would have to wait so I brought the journal and picked up some coffee and an onion bagel beforehand. Want to get this down about what happened at the bakery before I forget . . .

While waiting for my bagel to be toasted and cream-cheesed, a father and his two girls were also waiting for their order. I noticed one of the girls was staring at me, perhaps she heard my deaf voice or noticed my hearing aids. The younger one had her nose up against the display case where multicolored cakes and pies revolved on glass shelves. She slapped her hand on the glass every time a cake circled past her nose.

The cashier wrapped my bagel in wax paper and rang up my order. When I turned to go, I noticed a sour odor and a murky puddle on the floor. The older girl had vomited. It must've happened very quickly. The father was already outside dabbing his daughter's mouth with a handkerchief. And she was still staring at me.

Sitting in my car outside the bakery, I couldn't help but wonder if the little girl was shocked by the sight of a deaf person. People not used to seeing a physical handicap can get ill or act repulsed by what they see or hear. My mother once told me that when she was in junior high school, they had a dance where everyone drew their dance partner's name out of a hat. My mother's partner was a girl with no arms; her hands were way up at the shoulder joints. Thalidomide poisoning. The girl's mother probably took it as a sedative during her pregnancy. What my mother had to do was hold this girl's little hands and dance. My mother became sick to her stomach and had to leave. She never came back to the dance that night.

I still think there are hearing people out there today that feel the same way when they see a deaf person for the first time in their lives. I've been told deafness is an invisible handicap, but I don't think that's always so. Sometimes people are stupefied at the sight of sign language exchanged between deaf people. Occasionally, deaf people will let out grunts, groans, and odd vocalizations that may be offensive to the ears of the hearing. Some may look alien as a result of a particular syndrome that causes deafness—Waardenburg or Treacher Collins, to name a few.

Well, here comes the clipboard lady. Let's hope she can maintain her composure. . . .

March 2022

Olives

"About time you tried something different," said Ilene. "All you like is beer, beer, beer. You need to expand your mind a little." Her hands made the shape of doors opening above her forehead. She pours the martini from a pitcher.

"I don't trust martinis," said Ryan. "What goes in them?"

"I don't know." Ilene took a sip.

"You've never had a martini before?"

"No. But I know that hearing people put green olives in them—yuck! You might as well drop a pat of butter in your drink."

"What about black olives?

"They're healthier. More like a vegetable."

"Is that why you asked for black olives?"

"Yeah, and to make it a deaf drink. Go on, try one." She plops another black olive in her drink.

"No thanks, I'm going to stay with the green ones."

"I'm telling you, the green ones are fake. They stuff those little red things inside them."

"Those are called pimentos," said Ryan.

"Whatever they are, I don't like them. They remind me of hearing people, sticking their little red tongues out, yakking away. Yak-yak-yak." She makes little back-and-forth tongue gestures like a dog panting.

"Ilene, that's not very nice!"

"You're too polite with hearing people. And, please don't sign my name—that's not Deaf culture."

"I'm not going to fight over this again. I want us to have a nice, quiet dinner." Ryan unfolds his linen napkin and spreads it over his lap.

"Fine!" She fishes out her olive and nibbles on it.

"So, how's the black olive make yours a deaf drink?"

"It looks different. It's black, solid. No holes. No red tongue. And it's tough in the middle, like it's got guts."

Ryan snorts. "Ok, whatever . . . ." He raises his drink to propose a toast. "To what?"

"A *different* anniversary," said Ilene.

"But this is our first anniversary."

"I know." She spits the pit into her hand and slips it in the space under the edge of her plate.

"So it'll be different no matter what," said Ryan.

"I know. Turn off your voice."

"How do you know I'm using my voice?"

"The veins are sticking out on your neck."

"I can't help it. It's a habit. I'm working on it." Tired of signing with one hand, Ryan sets his drink down.

"You're doing good. I really appreciate you're trying." She lifts her drink. "Happy anniversary."

Ryan lifts his glass again and looks at Ilene from across his glass rim. "Black, hmmm. Interesting."

Ilene squints her eyes and swallows. She mouths the word "whew."

"Whoa!" said Ryan. He clears his throat.

"That's a martini!" said Ilene.

"Tastes like gasoline."

"I love it. So powerful."

"No more for me. That's it," said Ryan.

"I feel a slight buzz already. You?"

"Too dangerous," said Ryan.

"Only live once."

"I have to drive."

"Then, I'll do all the drinking." She gulps the last of her drink and pours herself another one. "So . . . do you want to have a discussion?"

"To discuss what?"

"Oh . . . discuss us."

"What's there to discuss?"

"I'd like to know what's going to become of us."

"We're in a relationship—it's good."

Ilene picks a black olive from the little white bowl and sucks on it. She toys with it in her mouth.

"What do you mean become of us?" said Ryan.

"Do you see anything in the future for us?" She signs without moving her lips, shifting into her deaf-deaf mode.

"I don't have a crystal ball like . . . I see . . . I see . . . us getting married . . . with three kids . . . a farmhouse . . . I don't know. That's hard."

"Don't you have any idea or, you know?" said Ilene.

Ryan downs the rest of his martini. "Arggh! Whew. That burns." Ilene pours him another glass.

"I mean we've known each other, what, twelve months now?"

"Twelve months!?"

"What're you looking at your watch for? She quickly spits out the olive pit and puts it under her plate. "Hey . . . hey, look at me . . . ." She nudges him hard.

"Don't do that here."

"I wanted your attention."

"It's not polite. We're in a restaurant."

"That's Deaf culture," said Ilene.

"In a hearing restaurant, no!"

"Want me to yell for your attention?"

"No."

"I can yell."

"No. Not polite."

"It's the Deaf way."

"It's rude."

"What do you want me to do?"

"Just slide your hand across the table and softly say, 'Excuse me.'"

"I'm not going to talk," said Ilene.

"You can."

"No, I can't."

"You don't want to, that's why."

"That's right, it's my choice."

"You were willing to yell a minute ago. What's the difference?"

"I prefer not to use my voice, okay?"

"But you said you wanted to yell."

"I did not. I said, 'Do you want me to yell?'"

"That's it. That, that," said Ryan, pointing at her sign for YELL.

"Is that what you want?"

"Yes, that's it. That. You just said it. You asked, 'Do you want me to yell?'"

"<u>Do</u> you want me to yell?"

"Yes, that's the one."

"I'm asking <u>do</u> you want me to?" said Ilene.

"NO! Of course not."

"Okay, then."

"Obviously, you were willing to use your voice."

"No. You have a good voice, I don't."

"Oh, sheesh. Well, I'm willing to be more deaf-deaf when I'm alone with you."

"Okay, fine. Let's see you be more deaf-deaf."

"But when we go out, like to this fancy restaurant here, we need to have manners, not deaf manners."

"What do you mean 'deaf' manners? You make it look negative."

"Not negative. I respect Deaf culture where it congregates. But in a place like this, we have to follow the rules of hearing culture." He demonstrates. "Napkins on your lap, order drinks, followed by appetizers, main course, dessert, and leave a tip." Ryan takes a big gulp of his martini.

"Go on—deaf people leave tips!"

"Not the ones I know."

"You mean I have to adjust according to what culture I'm in?"

"That's our society," said Ryan.

"What do you mean by 'deaf manners' then?"

Ryan becomes more demonstrative. "Nudging other people hard, slapping the table, stomping your feet, waving your hands, yelling 'HEY!'" He snickers.

"What's so funny?"

"I just yelled out loud."

"You did?"

"Yes. Now the whole restaurant is watching."

"You really did yell?"

"Yes! You didn't see my veins?"

"That's what you call 'deaf manners'?"

"Yeah. That."

"I get it."

"You gotta conform," said Ryan. "Say you walk into a blues bar. Everybody in there is black. There's a live band playing blues music. You must follow their rhythm, their moods." He claps his hands rhythmically. You can't do all that deaf hand-waving, table-slapping, foot-stomping stuff while they're playing. Really spoils the blues mood. You know?"

"I know. That's common sense."

"What's common sense?"

"Yeah, it's common sense," said Ilene.

"What?? When you nudged me like that? You call that common sense?"

"Really, I didn't hit you that hard. I just touched you. You're exaggerating; you always do with everything I say."

"I'm going to pour myself another," said Ryan.

"Help yourself! Aren't you going to eat your olive? People tend to eat their olive after they drink a martini."

"Oh, you mean hearing people??"

"You know what I mean."

"Now, who's the one that's copying hearing people?"

"It's not copying. You do whatever you want."

"I don't know if I'm going to eat this or not. I'm going to leave it out."

"Wow! On the table? Are you sure that's good manners??"

"I'm going to be different. You watch."

"Hey, I thought you said before you weren't going to have another drink," said Ilene.

"After the initial shock, it doesn't taste so bad now. I feel a *different* kind of drunk."

"What do you mean 'a different kind of drunk?'"

"A sophisticated drunk."

"Yeah, a hearing drunk."

Spring 2003

The Horn

One night, Rusty is necking with his girlfriend on the sofa by the living room window that overlooks the apartment parking lot. It's a warm California evening. The windows are open, lights are out. Every now and then he opens one eye to look out the window to be sure all's right with the world.

Rusty and his girlfriend are both deaf. They've had fights over whether to call themselves *deaf* or *hard of hearing*. They leave their hearing aids on because they enjoy hearing their own lovemaking sounds.

Suddenly they hear this loud, continuous sound. They stop and look at each other. Somebody yelling? Nobody can hold a yell that long. A train? But there's no train around here. A foghorn? Ha! In a Southern California valley?

They slowly get up by the window and poke their heads between the curtains, their naked butts hidden from the outside world. Lights start to come on in apartments across from them. A guy runs out of one of the apartments wielding a Bowie knife. People are coming out in their pajamas and bathrobes.

Rusty nudges his girlfriend and points to the guy with his Bowie knife. They both laugh at the seriousness of his expression. She points out the sixty-year-old landlady's Mickey Mouse bathrobe. They bury their faces into the sofa cushion stifling giggles. The loud, continuous sound drones on.

All of the neighbors close in on a row of cars on the lot. Rusty signs to his girlfriend that some jerk's car alarm probably got tripped. One of the neighbors goes to each car and puts his ear up close to the grill. He looks like a doctor listening to a patient's heart. Then they all gather around the white Chevy Impala with the bumper sticker that says, "I'm not deaf, I'm just ignoring you." Everyone looks up toward their window. They duck.

Rusty throws on some clothes and tells his girlfriend he'll be right back. He grabs his keys and heads straight to his car, ignoring everyone talking to him at once. He put his hand on the dashboard—that confirms the sound is indeed coming from his car. He jiggles the steering wheel spokes. The steering wheel has this rubbery portion that he pushes this way and that. The horn continues to blare on into the sleepy California night.

Finally, Rusty gets the brains to open his hood and yank out the horn's wires. Now he remembers how he got this horn problem. He had let it go all this time. Three weeks ago, while driving along Sunset Boulevard, he pressed on his horn for a long time at a wise guy in a yellow Cadillac convertible. The Cadillac cut right in front of his car, barely missing him. Rusty caught up and blasted him with the horn. The Cadillac driver practically went through his roof. When Rusty let go of the horn, that honking continued for the next five blocks. All of the shopkeepers and passersby stopped what they were doing and watched Rusty drive by. Rusty waved and smiled to everyone while discreetly joggling the horn spokes on the steering wheel with his other hand. He managed to get the horn unstuck by manipulating one of the spokes.

After that horn-awakening night with his girlfriend, Rusty takes his car to a shop to see how much it would cost to fix it. He wants it fixed because he loves the control the horn gives him over people who can hear. It shocks them. Makes them move out of the way. Makes them curse and gesture—all from lightly pressing this powerful little lever.

Rusty finds out it's way too expensive to have the horn repaired. He goes home and figures out a system. There are three places on the steering wheel designed to activate the horn—the spoke at three o'clock, a spoke at six o'clock, and one at nine o'clock. The three o'clock spoke won't even produce a sound. Forget that. The one at six o'clock will give him something but only when it feels like it, and when it does it'll get stuck. The one at nine o'clock works.

He'll just have to remember the nine o'clock spoke if he needs it in a moment of quick decision . . . or to provoke hearing people.

September–October 1996

The Ivoryton Inn
(*In memory of Dorothy Miles*)

Empty bar at the Ivoryton Inn, just the bartender, me, and the TV. The odor of stale cigarette smoke and beer clings to everything made of wood. This is the town where they used to ship elephant tusks up the river and forge them into piano keys.

The bartender is skinny with sunken cheeks, deep-set eyes. All he wears is black. He tries to strike up a conversation but I hear nothing; only see mumbling lips and CNN on the tube in the background.

So, I just nod.

Though no one has come in, he constantly wipes the bar. I order a glass of wine and when it comes, I make sure the glass stays on the coaster.

I lived upstairs in this place quite a few summers past to interview deaf theatre students from the world over. They came to this bar to eat, drink, and rehearse play scenes for drama school held in an old, renovated grist mill nearby.

Their silhouettes sit beside me, and some with drinks in their hands lean on the baby grand piano:

Shan from Hong Kong complains about the lack of opportunity for deaf actors in his country.

Anu from India isn't here to learn about acting but ways to meet American men and get a green card.

Loretta, the redhead from Australia—unaware that she has no stage presence—thinks her flashy personality will attract all sorts of Hollywood offers.

Tom from England studies a Pinter monologue and drinks milk; he tries out words in two-handed British fingerspelling.

As if it was just yesterday, I see their facial expressions and native sign languages, each with its own signature and syntax.

At one time in the early seventies, a deaf theatre company won a Tony Award. A sudden growing interest in hiring deaf actors came about. Hundreds and hundreds of eager deaf students enrolled in the

summer program, each one manufactured—some against their will—
to the specs of well-known acting teachers and directors from New
York City who could hear.

I finish my wine and leave a tip at the bar's edge. The bartender
gives me a shifty glance and then swoops in like a vulture to grab his
money and put the wine glass away. He wipes the entire bar again even
though a small area was smudged.

On the way out I touch the baby grand. My hand trails along the
curves, stopping at the keyboard. I strike a black key, an unknown
note, thinking about fabricated deaf actors. I tap a white key and
wonder about the elephants in Africa or India or wherever they were
caught.

What were these humble creatures feeling as the poachers drugged
and held them down to saw off their noble tusks?

2013

The Decree

On Jero the 7th in the year 3051, the World Intelligence Federation (WIF) secretly enacted a decree that would make the human race extinct. WIF—an organization enforcing international peace, security, development, human rights, and humanitarian affairs—determined that Earth had simply run out of room.

The decision was made after finally consenting to the fact that all of the other planets in the solar system were incapable of sustaining human life forms. Even Mars, the most likely planet thought to extend the human race, ended up becoming a vast money-pit wasteland—much like the Earth's moon. Funds for further exploration into other galaxies had run out—mostly what was left out there was a mobile collage of space junk: old satellites, outdated telescopes, empty cylinders of rocket boosters, and other aeronautical whatnots randomly crashing into each other, breaking off into smaller pieces and floating around like flotsam and jetsam. It had gotten to the point that any company shooting up spacecraft had to be sure to affix a sturdy separator on the capsule, a device akin to a cowcatcher on a locomotive—to push aside obstacles.

The deserts, prairies, and mountains of the world were covered with asphalt (or some form thereof) and were now overcrowded with metropolises. Nothing was made out of paper or wood anymore. The trees died off long ago. Hard-nosed environmentalists lost their thousand-year battle to save the last frontier from megacorporations. Even strips of land left by the ever-receding oceans were bought and covered with global franchises and were now riddled with aging desalination plants. Businesses were built on concrete pillars, extending far over the seas with the knowledge that with time, water would wane and ready-made parking lots would emerge. Of course, later after the black-tops were rolled on, the parking areas became lined and divided into narrow spaces for the one-person aircrafts that had become so popular.

When WIF met every year during Jero on hotel-ridden Mount Everest, they always checked in under the auspices of an international grass-skiing organization. Everest boasted of having the longest and softest grass slopes in the world, thanks to a new hybrid of blue-green grass called Cyanoturf™. Everest also prided itself on having the fastest magnetic-vertical-levitation elevators at its core.

As a result of the depleted ozone layer, the extra month of Jero was added to the world's calendar last year to give an extra month of presummer—a time between spring and summer in the northern hemisphere when the weather was consistently warm but not so hot as to call it summer and not too cool to be spring. For those in the southern hemisphere, it gave them an extra month of autumn to enjoy before winter sets in.

For security and confidentiality purposes, WIF employed a communication system called VISUNO, a sign language that based many of its signs on handshapes from every country, in addition to some newly created gestures to satisfy their own parliamentary lingo. To ensure that all members stayed within the bounds of gestural rules and grammar, WIF always employed a parliamentarian who was deaf and fluent in the sign languages of the world and the international gestures popular among Deaf societies, never mind that deaf and hard of hearing people have dwindled to a smattering few around the globe— They were maintained and preserved like special animals until they went extinct.

Ericson John Mahfood, or Mahf as his contemporaries knew him, was at the spry old age of 125, and on his last legs—wheels actually—since his main form of mobility was by wheelchair hovercraft. People always knew whenever he approached because of air hissing from the narrow space between the ground and his wheelchair. The hovering was like the barely floating puck in the ancient game of air hockey.

Mahf joysticked his way to the head of the United Nations-like round table and parked himself next to the elected moderator for the year, a 115-year-old woman from Quebec who happened to be born blind. The retinal transplants she received as a child totally restored her vision. Mahf secretly envied her because he was still profoundly deaf despite his government-controlled cochlear implants. Mahf, being from the US, heard patriotic slogans and government ads all day long on a loop that his brain could not turn off. It wasn't like the battery-operated hearing aids of yore where one could simply flick the "off" switch and enjoy complete silence from the cacophonies of life. Ironically, in addition to restoring hearing, cochlear implants were designed to eliminate head noise, but the robotic-voiced slogans were like a self-induced tinnitus.

The most recent meeting went unusually well. Mahf wasn't called on to clarify anything parliamentary. The committee skimmed over world problems and concentrated on one surefire solution. It was time to stop human reproduction.

Mahf raised his hand for the first time that day. He ignored the Pizza Hut commercial that was running along his auditory nerve and focused on what he wanted to say. "Point of clarification: 'Cease human reproduction?'" He made the gesture for "coitus" and then the slit-throat sign for "stop."

The room was quiet; nobody moved. The moderator looked over at Mahf. He could see the blue of the fake retinas reflecting from the back of her eyes. She nodded her head to confirm.

Then, she proceeded: "Starting from January 1st, 3052, all newborn infants will be vaccinated with a virus that ceases sperm and egg production as well as sex drive."

"Why?" Mahf drew a big question-mark gesture in the air.

"May I remind you that as parliamentarian, it is not your job to question the decisions of the committee?" said the moderator. Her hand movements were rough and jerky—an ongoing problem that doctors still had not resolved with centenarians.

Mahf made the classic "hear-no-evil, see-no-evil, speak-no-evil" gesture, and spun around back to his place in the circle.

"To reiterate," said the moderator, "since most marriages ended in divorce, it was the WIF's decision to make people sexless and lead individual, independent lives until they expire. Since cryopreservation has been banned, we have begun the shutdowns of cryogenic labs worldwide. WIF forces will extract, thaw, and properly dispose of cryopreserved human specimens. From here on out, no one is allowed to freeze their bodies for the future."

Mahf remembered reviewing the previous meeting's minutes on video. He realized it was not a drastic measure, for people, by nature, were quite self-centered anyway. If the pleasure of sex was absent, how would they know what was missing at infancy? People would read and

hear about sex in the past, but not with longing. It would be like looking at a photograph of a pink Cadillac from the 1950s or of a drive-in
movie theatre landscape. And, who wants to defrost and deal with a
fat, ugly, wrinkled billionaire? Thousands of years down the road, who
would care? Or millions of years, for that matter?

The committee calculated that when the human race gradually
becomes extinct, Mother Earth would need two million years to
replenish herself and begin life again.

The plan would be to have the WIF scientists begin the search for
people with the highest IQs in their respective ethnic and cultural
groups. Drawings were underway to design and build a humongous,
durable time capsule to hold an underground laboratory that contains
a cold room and life support systems. The sperm and egg cells from
a male and a female of each group were to be extracted and preset
for conception, in which a solar timer would trigger the release at the
right time. Rows of biomechanical yet lifelike wombs would be set and
ready for insemination and the nine-month human gestation period.

"Mr. Mahfood, would you kindly introduce to the committee your
idea of the language capsule?" asked the moderator.

Mahf wheeled forward and pressed a button to elevate his seat
for better visibility . . . and attention. He pressed a combination of
keys on his wheelchair to call up a 3-D holographic display appearing
beside him.

"I've put together a language packet for the reborns after the regenesis of the world," This packet comes in the form of soft robots with
electroluminescent skin of elastic polymer allowing maximum flexibility
and color in facial expressions. To create a three-dimensional, gestural
language that would become a visual Esperanto of sorts for the new
world, the robots would be programmed to express the full range of
motions of gestures and a vocabulary of 1,650 morphemes. This would
become the universal language of the new world. As soon as babies are
born, these robots will begin exposing them to VISUNO. Any questions?" Mahf punctured the air with a big question mark gesture.

A WIF member raised his hand. He was the oldest member of WIF,
a 132-year-old man from China who managed to stay healthy on a
daily diet of tofu and tai chi. He stroked the thin tendrils of his mustache before posing his question in VISUNO.

"Suppose one of the reborns begin to utter sounds and start using that as a basis to form a new language?"

"What?? Did you miss the video memo or fall asleep during the committee's discussion about genetic engineering?" Mahf gestured.

The moderator shot Mahf a glance. Again, he saw the blue retinal reflections of her eyes give him a sharp, invisible sting of admonishment. He didn't care. His kind was becoming extinct. What did he have to lose by being honest and forthright? Besides, everybody's gonna die.

Mahf took a deep breath. "Reborns will not have vocal cords. They're being gene-spliced out. Too much noise pollution and misunderstandings with spoken language. More questions?"

Fu Manchu'ed shook his head, bowed in thanks, and sat down.

Next, the moderator reconfirmed with the committee that scientists would select certain flora and fauna that would contribute the most to world regeneration. Pollination pods containing the seeds of flowers, trees, and vegetables would be buried in strategic locations around the globe. This also went for breeding pods for animals and insect groups and their reproductive samples along with equipment to facilitate and germinate. Everything was dependent entirely on solar energy since it is known that the sun will be a constant energy source for at least another five million years. What would be particularly significant for regenesis was the inclusion of the hardiest invasive species that would help break up the proverbial concrete seal around the world: cockroaches, rats, pigeons, kudzu, and tree-of-heavens.

And then, the moderator summarized, a new society would form without a basis for egocentricity or prejudice. Mahf pressed a button on his wheelchair to lower himself, for he had forgotten that he had remained elevated during his language pod spiel. He laid down his head over his arm, which was resting on the front wheelchair panel, to try to muffle what was coming. There was just no way he could block out the Coca-Cola commercial that was jingling its way through his Bluetoothed ear implant.

June 2021

The Rockers

On an island visited by many people (thirty-some years ago) stands the Rising Sun: an aging, grand hotel overlooking the sea. Cobwebs drape the beveled-glass entrance door, and through the spider-threaded veil is a tall, mahogany desk. An antiquated clipboard-pen set and hurricane lamp wait for guests: "PLEASE REGISTER HERE."

The old, hard of hearing man backs away from peering through the door and swallows hard. He slips his hand into his shirt pocket to turn up his hearing aid. He fastens the top button of his overcoat and tries the doorknob. He could hear it rattle when turned, but it was locked. Of course, what did he expect—an open invitation?

He walks along the wraparound porch to a window on the side of the hotel lobby, the wood creaking with his footsteps. He wipes the salt mist off a portion of the glass with his coat sleeve. A dark, portentous oil portrait, painted with no highlight in the eyes, hangs crooked on the wall behind the desk. He remembers this portrait with the perpetual stare that followed him from the main door to the picture window overlooking the shore.

The man walks cautiously down the wide porch to the back deck, mindful of the curled-up boards and pushed-up nails. He needs to see this every year on this day because this is where it all ended . . . for him.

Along the deck rests the day's only occupants: wooden rocking chairs, an Amish-like community absorbing the Atlantic spray; hard, quiet, sunburned, separate, fastened to customs and rules.

The man pushes one of the rockers. Instead of the smooth rocking motion he was expecting, it wobbled. He still can't remember which chair it was.

The man walks over to another rocker. Was this the one? He gives it a nudge. One of the spindle supports falls out and lands with a clatter on the deck. The amplified sound startles him, and he steps back quickly, looking up and down the porch. Silly. What's he looking for? Someone to arrest him for pushing a chair? He turns his hearing aid volume down a bit. He goes to a chair down by the end, one that looks sturdy, and eases himself onto it.

He looks out and sees the sky subtly pulling down its dusky-blue shade. Down below, on the dirt road that leads to a boat launch, a streetlight flutters as electrical surges ignite mercury vapors. And far off to the right of the launch is a jetty with a landmark beacon at its end that blinks off and on continuously.

A foghorn with a lonesome moan begins the nightlong, intermittent cycle. The man leans back in the chair and begins to rock. Even with the 40 decibel loss in both ears, he can still hear and enjoy the horn's prolonged, low-frequency blasts. He remembers hotel guests from the past complaining about being kept up at night by the all-night warning. He always told them he found it soothing and it put him to sleep.

The chairs inhale the cool, moist salt air and gently sway to the ebb of twilight. The floorboards pick a raspy tune punctuated by groans from rusty nails.

The man takes a pill out of his coat pocket and looks at it a long time. Then, he puts it in his mouth. The capsule immediately sticks to what little moisture is on his tongue. He leaves it there for a little bit until enough saliva builds up. He swallows the pill and closes his eyes.

The foghorn wail drifts by again. An Acadian rocker (acquired from an antique store in Bar Harbor) with a sturdy but splintered oak frame leans back and smiles at an old memory: an early spring day with the sun drawing steam from the gnarled platform wet with morning dew. The innkeeper's cat slinked by leaving paw prints and then came around under the rocker's seat. The slightly cross-eyed Siamese stretched and sharpened its claws on one of the four ornately carved legs, sending cold chills up the chair's spindled back. The rocking chair—with its cleft feet firmly planted in long, tapered runners—rolled hard over the thoughtless cat's tail, hoping to put a kink in it. Day after day of shed fur and hairballs all over the seat was absolutely disgusting. And that repulsive purring. No, not purring—the phlegmy snore of an overweight man.

The other chairs nod, recalling the feline's fateful day (and what an ear-piercing caterwaul).

The man stops, opens his eyes and turns his head to the right, sensing someone or something moving on the other chairs. His vision swirls, and when it settles he doesn't see anything except the silhouettes of the rockers facing the ocean. He turns his head back and closes his eyes again and rocks.

An old New England fiddleback, transported from the piano room of a Victorian mansion in Essex, recollects a long-ago evening when a teenager with muddy sneakers jumped on her newly varnished seat. The pimply young man grabbed her weak back and swung wildly, whooping his head off. The rubber treads on his soles made horrible sucking sounds while cramming mud between her softwood slats. Finally, unable to withstand the filth any longer, she tipped herself back and bucked the bewildered boy against the outside hotel wall.

The line breaks. The chairs snicker at the memory of the fourteen-year-old pell-melling through the air.

Again, the man stirs at the sound of wood on wood but ignores the source. Instead, he stops and looks up at the night sky through half-closed eyes for comfort. He sees Orion, the hunter, filled out in flesh between the stars. Orion's legs are moving toward some destination, perhaps toward Eos, his lover, the goddess of dawn. The man resumes his swaying to and fro.

A rustic Bentwood found intact—with bark and twig scars—on the back porch of a deserted home in the Adirondacks remembers a Fourth of July weekend—ruined by a two-year-old. The girl's mother plopped her down on the chair and left her to eat a double-dipped strawberry cone. Moments later, the clumsy child knocked a scoop of ice cream onto the intricately woven cane seat. She began to bawl even though another scoop was left. The girl leaned forward and tried to slide off to tell her mother what happened. The chair refused to budge. It was as if the chubby kid were stuck in a high chair. Trapped, she howled until a grown-up came to the rescue.

The chairs chuckle to and fro at the Bentwood's recollection. They nudge one another at how surprising it was that their fragile friend had mustered the courage to stand her ground.

A warm, southerly wind blows over the veranda, sweeping away the fog. The man struggles to lift open an eye—the lid feels like lead. A blue-black tinge in the sky outlines the horizon. The foghorn wails again and the beacon signals continuously. The man's eyelids get heavier and heavier and then close.

Two Shaker slat-backs, handmade the same week by a Mennonite cabinetmaker, hurriedly tap their rockers for attention. It is getting close to daybreak—remember the beautiful elderly couple? The sweet hearing-impaired man and his wife who had cancer? The chairs swing solemnly.

Holding her tenderly by the arm, the gentleman escorted his wife out to the deck every morning. He eased her onto the simple, elegant chair she loved and spread a patchwork quilt over her legs. He went back inside to buy hot drinks to ward off the morning chill.

Wrinkled like the grain pattern, the woman's fingertips caressed the chair's worn-smooth arms and came to rest on the mushroom knobs at the end. She leaned back and turned her head to the side. The sweet smell of maple brought a faint smile to her lips. How peculiar that an aroma could conjure, all at once, so many memories: their gingerbread-trimmed house in the country, raking leaves with her grown son, swinging with her granddaughter on her lap—her hands suddenly clutched the palm-sized knobs. Her face contorted. A tear rolled off her cheek and seeped into wooden pores. The chair rocked delicately.

In the hotel restaurant, the cook always prepared a batch of hot cocoa at seven in the morning. "None of that instant, artificial slop," the innkeeper would say to his cook; "those two come here each year as if they are on their first honeymoon, and they're the perfect touch to our seaside resort." Walking away, he would turn and add, "They cause no problems, so treat them like fine china, yes?"

The cook took out a couple of handcrafted mugs with seashell imprints and filled them with the steaming beverage. Next, he topped off the drinks with real whipped cream and bittersweet chocolate shavings.

Hearing the screen door kick open, the woman quickly wiped her eyes. Her husband pulled his rocker alongside hers so that their chair arms rubbed one another. They held hands, smiling, rocking slowly and easily as the ocean introduced a new dawn.

North along the shoreline, the man saw a great blue heron take off from behind a tuft of sea grass. The bird, flying in a low and graceful arc, skimmed the crest of a breaking wave. The woman's hand tightened on her husband's and then loosened for the last time. His head jerked from a quick, puncturing pain on his knuckles. Her arm fell.

His gaze returned to the back of his hand where dark-pink, crescent impressions, left by her fingernails, faded from his skin. Gingerly, he picked up his wife's limp hand. Not ready to look at her face, he slowly twirled the diamond ring that he slipped on her finger forty-eight years ago at the altar.

An orange-magenta glow blooms over the water. At the far end of the porch, the man slumps in his chair. The beacon blinks off and on. The foghorn releases its last warning for the night, a last call of assistance even though it can't prevent a collision that may take place at sea; just like the old man's hearing aid emitting high-pitched feedback from the earmold hanging loose out of his ear, it can't help him hear and make things right again.

In daylight, the rocking chair clan remains still, but when nightfall comes, the surf will roll, crash, and spew shells and seaweed, leaving behind the day's high-tide mark. Then, the mist will creep past the shore up to the hotel. The deck will creak, and a rocking chair will rock, slowly, back and forth, back and forth.

Summer 2021

Acknowledgments

Although some of the pieces have been updated and revised, I wish to graciously thank the following publications in which my writings originally appeared:

Essays

"Southernmost Point." *Saw Palm: Florida Literature and Art*, Spring (2022). http://www.sawpalm.org/.

"Life Is Short: Autobiography as Haiku." *Washington Post*, October 28, 2001, F1 (now titled "The Honeybee Epiphany").

"Kindergarten to College—A Personal Narrative." Copyright 1991 from *Deaf Students in Post-Secondary Education*, ed. Susan B. Foster and Gerard G. Walter. Reproduced by permission of Taylor & Francis Group, LLC, a division of Informa plc.

"The Face of Grace." *Urbanite* (December 2006): 25.

"Day 57—On the Road with the National Theatre of the Deaf." *Uncharted* 5, no. 4 (Fall 1990): 4–8.

"From Lipreading Ants to Flying over Cuckoo Nests" originally appeared in *American Theatre* 18, no. 4 (April 2001). Used with permission from Theatre Communications Group.

"5 Things a Visual Dramaturg Looks for That Might Surprise You." *Avant Bard*, October 18, 2014.

"America Needs More Visual Theatre!" *Opening Stages* (March 2005): 10–12.

"Hearing the Same Message." *Griller* program, Center Stage (1999): 16–17.

"The Loneliest Game in the World." *Hearing Health* (Summer 2001).

"Island of Intrigue." *Inbetween Magazine* (February 1984): 20–22.

"Untitled." In *Stages of Transformation: Collaborations of the National Theatre Artist Residency Program*, ed. Charlotte Stoudt. Copyright © 2005. Published by Theatre Communications Group. Used by permission of Theatre Communications Group.

"Warm and Inspiring." *NTID Focus* (Fall 1986): 19. Reprinted with permission from the Fall 1986 issue of *NTID Focus* Magazine, a publication of the National Technical Institute for the Deaf at Rochester Institute of Technology. All rights reserved.

"Bicyclists Welcome." *Baltimore Sun*, March 10, 2002, 3R. First published in the *Baltimore Sun*.

"Mushrooms." *Carte Blanche* 41 (Spring 2021). https://carte-blanche.org/articles/mushrooms/.

"The Power of Salt Air." *Carolina Quarterly* 62, no. 2 (Fall 2012): 26–31.

"Boathouse, Westerly, RI." *Folio* 26, no. i1 (Spring 2011): 78–83.

"House in Savage." *Folio* 26, no. i1 (Spring 2011): 78–83.

"Little House on the Suburban Prairie," *Folio* 26, no. i1 (Spring 2011): 78–83.

"Watergraphs: *Deal Island House, Evaporating Street Lamp, Walking on Water, Parking Lot Clouds.*" *Northwest Review* 50, no. i03 (Spring 2021): 120–22.

"Anchored at Inner Harbor." *Mud Season Review*, no. 53 (December 20, 2020). https://mudseasonreview.com/2020/12/creative-nonfiction-issue-53/.

"The Psychic Cat Vendor." *Isotrope* (Spring 2022): 59–60. https://www.flcc.edu/academics/creative-writing/program-highlight.cfm.

Playlets

"Disconnected," Lamia Ink! 8th Annual One-Page Play Festival, New York, January 30–31, 1998.

"Remains of Bosnians" was performed by Willy Conley in the Holzman Gallery at Towson University on December 12, 1995.

"The Practice of Medicine" was performed by the author in the Holzman Gallery at Towson University on December 12, 1995. A revised version of the piece was later performed in the Kellogg Conference Center at Gallaudet University as part of the Deaf Entertainment and Arts Festival in June 1997.

"The Deaf Chef." In *Vignettes of the Deaf Character and Other Plays*, 55–58. Washington, DC: Gallaudet University Press, 2009.

"Dialogue of the Deaf—A Cultural Sight Bite," *Santa Ana River Review* 7, no. i1 (Spring 2021). https://sarreview.ucr.edu/dialogue-of-the-deaf-a-cultural-sightbite/.

"Citizenship." In *Vignettes of the Deaf Character and Other Plays*, 236–41. Washington, DC: Gallaudet University Press, 2009.

"Toxic Flower" was the winning selection in the 2023 Deaf Spotlight Short Play Festival at 12th Avenue Arts, Seattle, Washington.

Stories

"Every Man Must Fall." In *The Deaf Way II Anthology*, ed. Tonya M. Stremlau, 171–88. Washington, DC: Gallaudet University Press, 2002.

Acknowledgments

"A Photographic Memory," *Kaleidoscope—An International Magazine of Fine Arts, Literature, and Disability*, no. 18 (Winter/Spring 1989): 16–18.

"Characters in El Paso." In *Deaf American Prose*, ed. Kristen Harmon and Jennifer Nelson, 190–97. Washington, DC: Gallaudet University Press, 2012.

"The Seawall." In *No Walls of Stone: An Anthology of Literature by Deaf and Hard of Hearing Writers*, ed. Jill Jepsen, 39–44. Washington, DC: Gallaudet University Press, 1993.

"The Ear." In *Deaf American Prose*, ed. Kristen Harmon and Jennifer Nelson, 190–97. Washington, DC: Gallaudet University Press, 2012. Reprinted in *Tripping the Tale Fantastic*, ed. Christopher Jon Heuer, 21–34. Minneapolis, MN: Handtype Press, 2017.

"The Label." In *This Is What America Looks Like: Poetry and Fiction from DC, Maryland and Virginia*, ed. Caroline Bock and Jona Colson, 197–98. Washington, DC: Washington Writers' Publishing House, 2021.

"Sifting Dirt." *The Tactile Mind* (Winter 2002–2003): 12–19; reprinted in *Daring to Repair Anthology,* ed. Heather Tosteson and Charles D. Charles, 221–26. Decatur, GA: Wising Up Press, 2012; also reprinted in *Deaf Lit Extravaganza* ed. John Lee Clark. Minneapolis, MN: Handtype Press, 2013.

"Toxic Waste." *Vagabonds: Anthology of the Mad Ones* 10 (March 2022): 44–45.

"Olives." *The Tactile Mind: Earnest* (Spring 2003): 33–39. Adapted from a play under the same name and published in *Hearing Health* 14, no. 6 (November–December 1998): 40–41. The play was produced at the 10th Annual NeWorks Theatre Festival at the New Theatre in Boston, MA, January 15–30, 1999.

"The Horn." *Hearing Health* 12, no. 5 (September–October 1996): 9–10.

"The Ivoryton Inn." In *Deaf Lit Extravaganza*, ed. John Lee Clark, 109–11. Minneapolis, MN: Handtype Press, 2013.

"The Rockers." *The Scores*, no. 10 (Summer 2021). https://thescores.org.uk/willy-conley/.

Extra special thanks to Katie Lee, who inspired and encouraged me to assemble this collection. Your guidance and care were much appreciated. Thank you to Deirdre Mullervy for putting the finishing touches on the manuscript. And, as always, much gratitude to my wife, Ingrid, for sharing your artistic eye and linguistic touch to help make this a better book.